SEE ME: An Almost Autobiography

Lee Campbell

William Cornelius Harris Publishing

In collaboration

With

London Poetry Books

ISBN 978-1-911232-52-0

William Young

34 Birchwood Close, Bordesley Road SM4 5NH

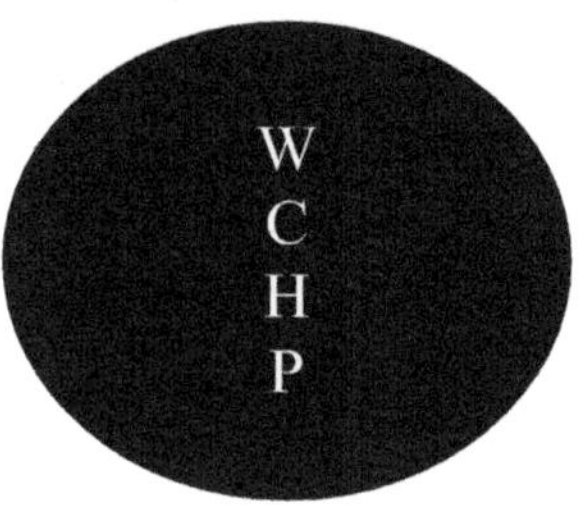

London Poetry Books

CONTENTS **Page**

CHAPTER 1: PEEPING AND HIDING

CHAPTER 2: CRUISING AND BRUISING

CHAPTER 3: SEEN AND FOUND

EPILOGUE

LIST OF ILLUSTRATIONS

Cover illustration: Pencil drawing of Rufus (2019)
All illustrations by Lee Campbell.
There are accompanying poetry films for all the poems in this collection.
You can view these online here:
www.filmfreeway.com/leecampbell

Connect with Lee
Instagram, X (formerly Twitter), Facebook: @leejjcampbell

CHAPTER 1: PEEPING AND HIDING

CLEVER AT SEEING WITHOUT BEING SEEN

Eye, I,
eye, I

Discover the same other
whilst under the cover

Creeping seeping peeping
covert operations
my teenage fascinations
awkward altercations
with non queer populations

Sensations that taught me
if ever they caught me
side cautiously er
deliberately blur words that infer derogatory slur

I got very clever
very clever at seeing without being seen.

UNCHARTED (THE CARTOGRAPHER)

Teenager in Nineties' Britain, always had in my hand,
a pencil to make drawings, to help me understand,
the world I was born into, which felt like foreign land,
because my sexuality was not what they had planned

Me drawing in a straight world, but mine was gay instead,
I made drawings in secret, hid them under my bed
I drew the world I longed for, imagined in my head,
I wished my world where men loved men was not in graphic lead.

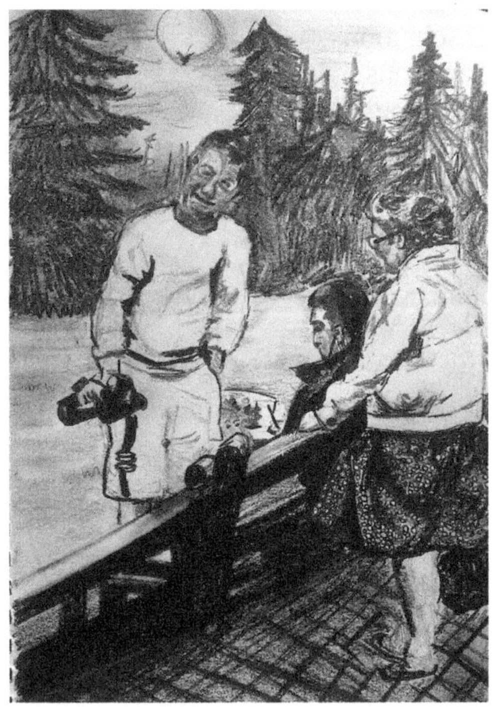

Figure 1
Pencil drawing from photograph of me drawing aged 19 with Nanny Joan looking over my shoulder with Dad standing with his camcorder (1997)

TACKLE

Nineties' football. Chelsea game
Me and Dad. Loved it same
Both loved tackle. Different name
Player's tackle. Felt no shame
'Dad I'm gay'. Out it came
Tried to hide. Tried to tame
Downplay gay. Felt to blame
All Dad say was 'Cut it out'

People pleaser. My mate Dan
Diamond geezer with a tan
Hid his thoughts about what I am
Hid he's bi from his old man
Gunners' tackle. Arsenal fan
Night they won. His white van
Kissed his lips. Out he ran
Cut me off and cut me out

Queerness fucks society
How it constructs what men should be
Naked woman on Page 3
She is not my cup of tea
Teenage scrapbook fantasy
Rather look at David B
In his kit, Man U F.C.
Get my scissors. Cut him out

Chelsea, Man U, match play draw
David Beckham, about to score
Saw his tackle, dropped my jaw
Dad went ‘GOAL!’, I went ‘PHWOAR!’
Chelsea 1, Beckham 4
Hear the crowds, hear them roar
Could not see what’s in store
‘Ref, you blind? Cut him out!’

Homophobe had his shot
Hooligan, out his cot
Swore at me, F-bomb drop
Effing queer, I am not

Half a brain, you ain’t got
Love my football never stop
Football snap, tackle, pop
Football cannot cut me out!

HEAD BOY

The weekly boys' cross-country run at school. Always last
Picking players for the football team. Always last
Towel stolen in the boys' showers. Always first
Out of school swimming club competition. Always first
Year 7 swimming every Tuesday
'How did *you* get to swim like *that*?' from a surprised bully
who later became Head Boy
Silver swimming medal followed but school bullies remained
Year 11 swimming every Friday
'How did *you* get to swim like *that*?' from Head Boy, early 1995
The bullies disappeared but my joy was placed elsewhere
In me catching a glimpse of Head Boy naked in the changing room
Only before had I seen such a sight on late night BBC2, 1989
Watching alone in my bedroom,
sound mute as to not awaken parents next door
A young Rupert Everett, full frontal, *Another Country*
Black and white TV could not dilute the beauty of his manhood.

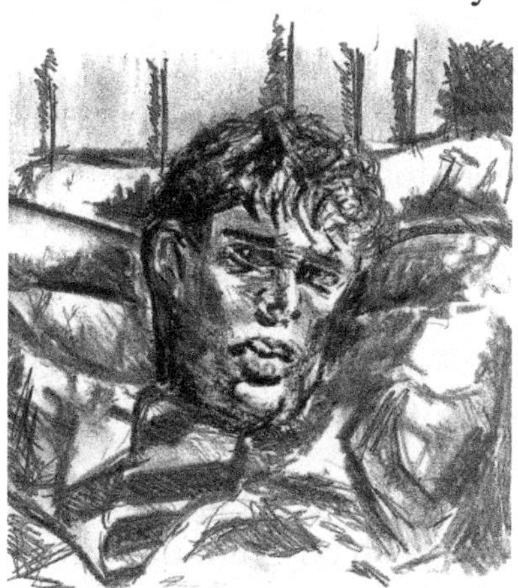

Figure 2 Pencil drawing of Rupert Everett in *Another Country* (1984)
Drawing made circa 1989/1990

POSH NOSH

State school in Nineties' Britain, near posh boys' private school
From working class background, those posh boys were so cruel
Laughed at Dad's Ford Cortina, my lower-class accent
For them a double no-no: I was common, I was bent
They shouted at me through the school gates,
'YOU DIRTY LITTLE QUEER!'
Went home and washed my hands with soap
to make them disappear

Me aged sixteen and naive
Didn't know then 'queer' meant 'gay'
Thought Nan meant she was Moby Dick,
'Came over a little queer', she'd say
They gave me dirty looks when I became erect
at sight of private school head boy but was that to deflect
not putting out their dirty on washing line to dry?
Whoever's dirty laundry can't hide in public eye

That film *Another Country*, two private schoolboys gay
Still bullied at my state school, but not in the same way
State school and school for posh boys
shared playing field for sports
Who knew it be a posh boy first give me dirty thoughts?

State school and school for posh boys shared same changing room
Me catching a glimpse of posh boy naked in the changing room

Forget *Another Country*, in end got upper hand
Speaking in gay Polari, posh boys not understand
For all the years of torture, wiping smirk off his smile,
me shouting Polari at him made posh boy run fast mile

'I wouldn't mind cleaning your kitchen mate!'
'Nothing like a bit of posh nosh'
'You keep bragging about your girlfriend's foofs
and how much you've got a Colin
tonight up her beef curtains
Cleaning her cage out
But I've seen you vada at me!
Wanting to put on the dish, tip the brandy,
tip the velvet, tip the ivy
Seen you through my bins, looking at my bene aris
It's you wanting to clean my kitchen
and to confirm what you keep telling me,
this little queer's kitchen is manky'

Posh boy be true to queer you,
don't hurt my mental health
You're only doing the dirty
the dirty upon yourself
Oh gosh, I like some posh nosh
but I will not clean up
my act for no posh boy, I'm proud,
me common queer as muck

And now that I'm that much older,
I know what I would do
I'd first clean out your kitchen mate,
then wash my hands of you!

CAMP (PART ONE)

Queering the landscape
Its points and angles creating a scene all of its own
Seemed so out of place in the shadow of mock Tudor terraces
But then strangely unapologetically making itself very at home

Awkward and not fitting in, like me at that time in the Nineties,
in my chalet, fancying my best mate's brother
At the end of the day, it may still have been Butlins
with certain views at odds with its neo-fantastical cover

The strangeness I felt of male redcoats singing ballads to teen girls
whilst informing my understanding then of what desire is about
This holiday camp where the camp was for straights
as campy redcoats were instructed by their bosses not to come out.

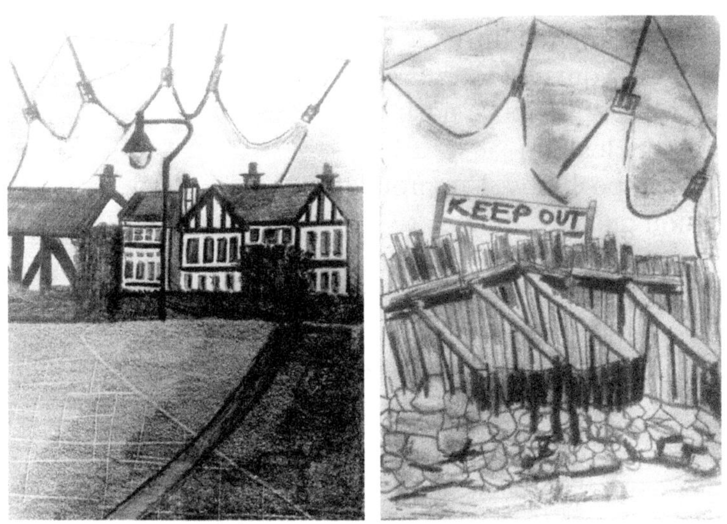

Figures 3 (left) and 4 (right)
Pencil drawing made circa 1990 of Butlins, Minehead

TOWEL TALE

Football showers. Dan hid my towel
School bully boy, he not my pal
So, I nicked his, nicked it somehow
He lucky boy, so well endow
The size of it made me think, 'WOW!'
I knew right then what I'm still now
I'm into boy, not into gal
I fancied Dave off *Emmerdale*
Made straight things gay. That Tory cow
Thatcher made straight white British male
hate all things homosexuelle

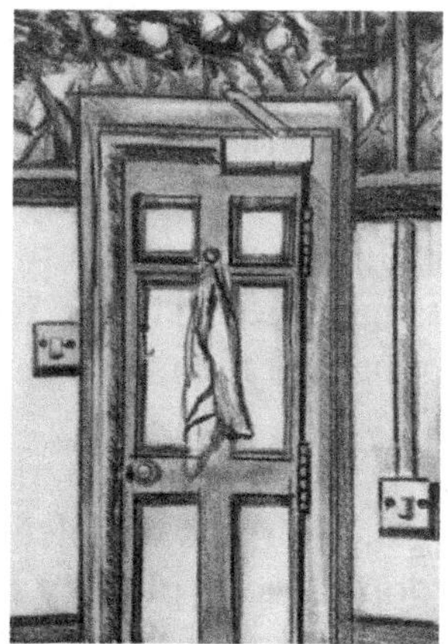

Figure 5 Pencil drawing made circa 1990 of Dan's towel on changing room door

One day, saw Dan, I raised my brow,
with mate Asif, getting a plough
Dan the convert, took Muslim vow
Hope Asif's meat, hope it's halal!
Bully Dan, 'holier than thou',
thought men like me should go to hell
You hypocrite! Hope girlfriend Mel
says, 'Dan, you're gay!' and then says,' Ciao!'.

BY GEORGE!

'Outside, the indecision, repetitive actions that got me one inch closer. Watch the door open and close and open and close. Wanted to experience the culture, the life, the very first pulse-stopping heart in my throat time. Couldn't even tell one person in my life what I was doing or where I was going. Thought my head was going to explode. I watch the door open and close and open and close ...'

the words of my friend Tim Kirk

Though Tim's bar was in New York and mine was in Brighton,
and our experiences twenty years apart, *by George!*
hearing his recollection was like listening to my own history
played back, almost word for word
Same fear, same anxiety, same risk that only gay men know
Despite the buzz, the thrill, the excitement mixed with dread,
only we know what's at stake the first time we enter
the super-ocularcentric world of the gay bar

It's 1990
Spending longer looking at Giorgios than learning his lyrics
I'm upstairs in my bedroom. Dad is playing Diana Ross downstairs
I like what I see on the back page of that week's *Look In* magazine
By Giorgios! Upside down, George Michael, you turn me, inside
out and round and round
Song lyrics printed over dark hairy chest
Lyrics become lines become words become hair
Hair loops and wraps around and through the holes of printed
letters through the 'o', the 'p', the 'd', and the 'e'

It's 1993
Spending longer looking at Italian stallion Giorgio
than paying attention to his Geography lesson
By Giorgio! Upside down, Mr Giorgio Suputo
Sir, you turn me, inside out and round and round

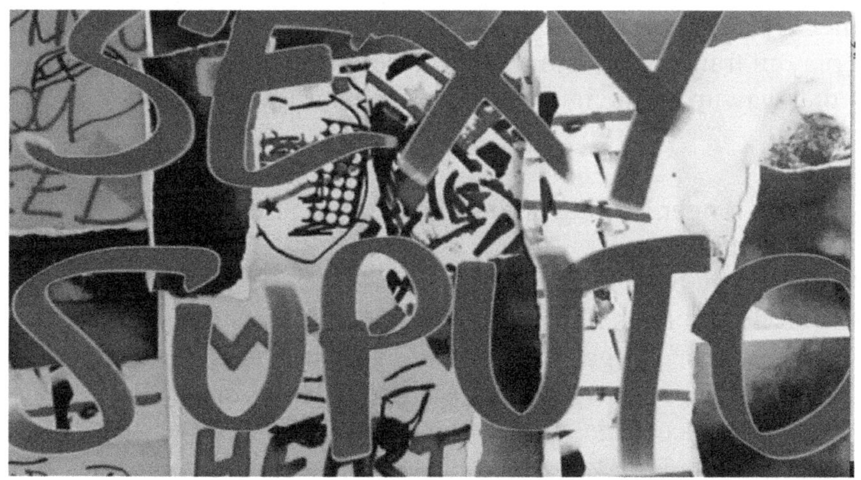

Figure 6
Still from poetry film *By George!* by Lee Campbell (2024)

It's 1996
Spending longer looking at fellow art school student George
than listening to him speak so conceptually about his sculptures during crits
By George! Upside down, George Taylor, you turn me, inside out and round and round

Thought at the time attending art school was about the art scene
Getting in. Until I realised it was all about me coming out

It's 1999
I'm in Berlin at the Georg Baselitz retrospective.
Spending longer looking at his painted male nudes than any other series on display
By Georg!
George Baselitz's well hung men hung well on gallery walls
when right way up meant upside down
A playful transgression in a world where upside down is turned wrong way up by the ignorant but dominant few

It's 2001
Spending longer looking at the sign George Street
than walking down it
Brighton, gay bar, Queens Arms
Heart a flutter. Legs like mush
The street was George, reminded of every previous crush
The stakes were high. Will I be accepted? Will I enter?
I pluck up the courage, deep breath. 3,2,1. Enter ...

'Jack Daniels and Coke please', I say to the barman
I put Diana Ross' *Upside Down* on the jukebox

By Giorgios! By Giorgio! By Georg! By George! I did it!
I've not been eaten alive by sharks
I spend the night drinking, dancing, flirting, kissing, being
Learning that bigger the fish, bigger the tackle!

QUEERO IN NERO

Bored in Caffè Nero
Music was so damn drearo
Male candy - nada, zero
But what pricked up my earo
My eyes then towards veero
Guy look like Richard Gereo
Short hair, had fight with shearo
He sat beneath a Miro
with book by Germaine Greero
Japan man named Akiro
served salad cavolo nero
These two lads then appearo
I knew that both were queero
As they kissed here in Nero
Thought how things changed round hereo
From when I lived in fearo
in Tunbridge Wells of yesteryearo
Folk maybe now see clearo
But memory don't disappearo
Remember this old dearo
I think her name was Vero
She gave me quite a sneero
Me peering at the rearo
of Natwest bank cashiero
I'd be imagineero
Swing him from chandeliero
Room Inn Hotel Premiero!
If cashier now were hereo,
I'd ask him, 'Fancy beero?'
If not gay, cry no tearo
I'd say, 'O.K. Cheerio'.

MY GREAT GREAT AUNTY ROSE

'A right piece of work', so the story goes
that's what Mum said or the truth she chose
about Mrs Jeffreys of Tunbridge Wells
Mum's great aunty, her Aunty Rose

Despite her rather dowdy clothes
and crooked teeth and her wonky nose
My great great aunty, Aunty Rose
looked rather sweet in old photos

Like parents, both tight so and so's
My great great aunty, Aunty Rose
hid her wages deep down belows
in depths of her silk pantyhose

My great great aunty, Aunty Rose
She loved French film, Francois Truffaut's
*Les Quatre Cent Coup*s (*The 400 Blows*)
And a poem or two she did compose

Behind her mask being morose
A dare devil was Aunty Rose
On husband's bike, on Uncle Joes
His motorbike, look, there she goes!

Go back and forwards, to's and fro's,
she loved to dance did Aunty Rose
Her Charleston step in stilettos
kept all the boys firm on their toes

In Nevill Park lived Aunty Rose
The street where tree, money tree grows
That part of town, no terrace rows
two up two down, like Aunty Flo's

My great great aunty, Aunty Rose
How afford live there, do you suppose?
She kept it quiet to not expose
In case her friends turned up on their nose
A live-in maid was Aunty Rose

For a wealthy Lord worked Aunty Rose
At a time when gay meant prison goes
One time whilst peeling potatoes
she caught Lord reading gay men's prose

Young teenage boys with feather bows
would go upstairs to his studios
'They come', Lord said 'to play dominos'
as his nose grew like Pinocchio's

Hamlet cigars puffed Aunty Rose
Killed by the smoke, her gravestone shows
Though with many folk, she came to blows
Did she mean good just misunderstood?
It's a shame now no one really knows

Now as it happens, as it goes,
when I was young, Mum's box of clothes
Put on her wig, strike a pose
And with flower hat, I was Aunty Rose!
The start of many alter-egos,
Campbell Camp-Belle, the name I chose.

CAMP-BELLE

My alter-ego, Lee Camp-Belle
She lights up a room but leaves a damp smell
Part hag, part drag, part fag in part
She has a sharp tongue but has a good heart
Some swear she's based on my friend Claire
The specs, the hair but not underwear
Camp-Belle is a mix of gender sorts
Pour femme perfume, male boxer shorts
Camp-Belle goes back to 1989
My primary school Christmas pantomime
I was one of the leads in *Cinderella*
with ugly sisters played by a fella
I was Monica
David was Nelly
Two camp divas made for the telly
Whilst David knew how to shimmy his hips,
I was getting used to having red on my lips
By opening night, I entered stage light
I looked quite the picnic in my stilettos and lipstick

One night in the dressing room, David told me he's gay
and that flirting with Prince was not just the play
It was obvious how David was chipper
when in this alternative version, Nelly's foot fits the slipper
I also had feelings not sure what then mind you
I know I got excited when the audience roared,
'Monica! Prince Charming, he's behind you!'
My moniker Monica taught me what it meant
to explore men as desirable without bullies calling me 'bent'
To see men in a new light and playfully flirt
To explore sexuality without getting hurt

Seeing gay men on telly, butch with moustaches
Seeing David effeminate, batting his lashes
These definitions of gay men for young me were distracting
but with Monica I explored and claimed it was acting
Eye up the Prince in front of a crowd
Mum and Dad in the audience, they were ever so proud
But what if they knew that the charming young Prince
made me not just my moniker more than just wince?

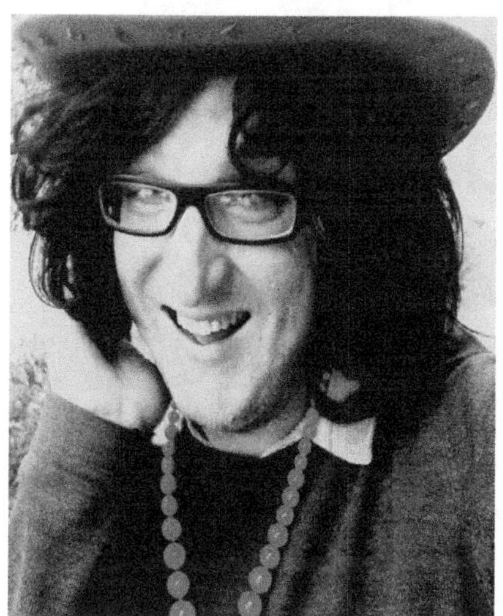
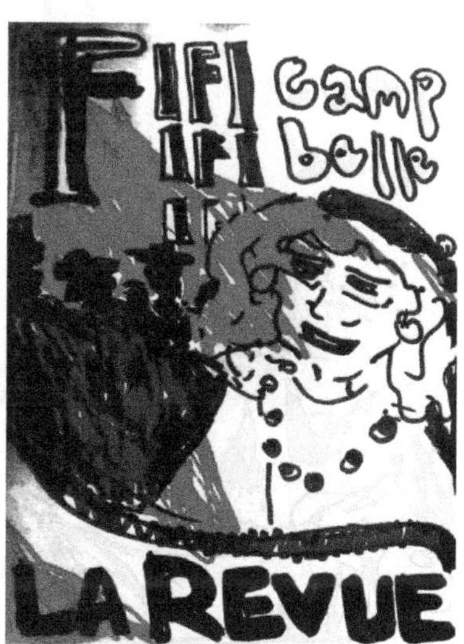

Figure 7 (left) Photographic portrait of me as Camp-Belle (2007)
Figure 8 (right) Felt-tip drawing of Camp-Belle (2007)

Many years later, I dressed up again
Camp-Belle just like Monica had an eye for the men
Me now in my late twenties, Camp-Belle was me
as the confident queer I once wanted to be
Her sharp tongue lashings and verbal bashings
Part dame, part fella, who's next for the kill?
No cartoon Cruella is Camp-Bella de Vil

The talk of the town in 2007
I then laid her to rest to cause trouble in Heaven
I'm now in my forties, young gays call me a 'daddy'
Miles away from Monica and a once confused wee laddie.

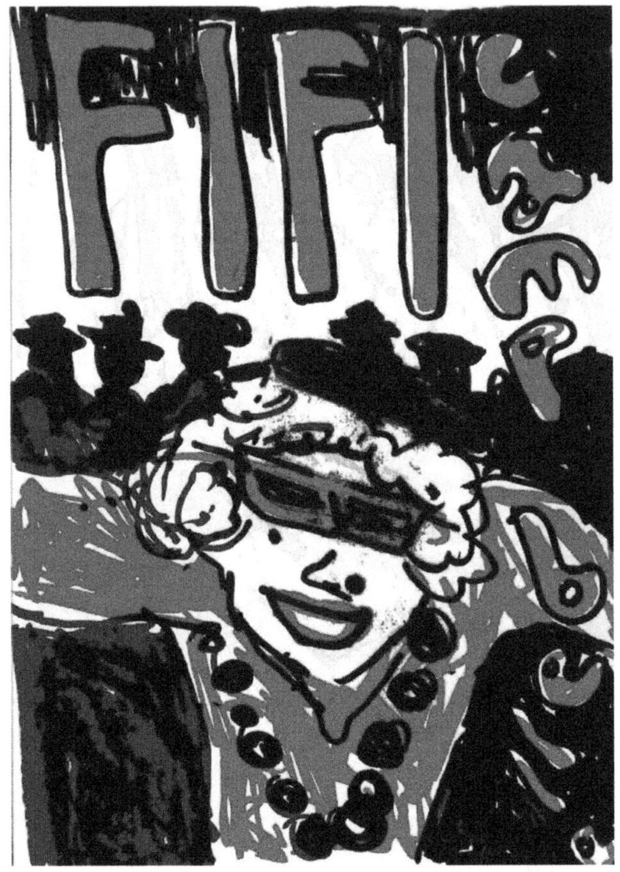

Figure 9 Felt-tip drawing of Camp-Belle (2007)

LITTLE SEEDS, BIG DREAMS

Sunflowers perfume, eau de toilette
Mum's favourite by Elizabeth Arden
When I catch its scent, the memory I get
is embarrassment in my mate's garden
In the Nineties, we both lived in rural Kent,
me in Pembury, Gary in the village of Marden
I once caught him gardening in the nude,
my good mate Gary Barden
Little seeds in me had been sewn by he
I said 'Ooh, I beg your pardon'
Gary's veg display gave to teenage me
unexpectedly a hard-on
When he asked if I liked what I did see,
I stumbled in me jargon
Out me coat, I got out my car key
Drove quick off in my Volkswagen
Shame I then went floppy, rather wilt
Schadenfreude, Freudeschaden
Little seeds, big dreams
When men in kilt,
I see beneath the tartan.

PERISCOPE

Climb aboard the 704 to Windsor
Great Grandad Ronald James is at the wheel
He drove the same Green Line bus
every day in the Forties and Fifties
Smog and chimneys gradually
replacing the Kent and Sussex countryside
Walked home alone at 1am from where he left his bus
at Woodbury Park Road in Tunbridge Wells
only to return a few hours later to begin the day's service
There and back, there and back, there and back

Grandad (his son, Ronald George) was told not to learn to drive
Mum (his daughter) was too nervous to learn to drive
Me and Mum got the Maidstone and District bus everywhere
Paid a flat fare for the Wanderbus ticket
Got off and on wherever we liked
Travelled to different counties in a day,
no more than five but more than three
Wanderbus wanderlust. Still be at home in time for tea
Straight to the upper deck of the double decker
Sat front seat on the right where there was a thing
of great wonder for me: the periscope

Day tripping with Mum, I was on a submarine
Intrigued by this rudimentary machine
Never quite sure if I was or not seen
I can still recall my fascination of the periscope
rather than name all the places I had been

The periscope - reflection and mirrors
Great grandad keeping one eye on his passengers

Those lads at the back upper deck having a smoke
Peer down the periscope, sometimes you see the driver
If he looks up, game over

Years later, I realised I enjoyed looking at men
Life for me then was playing periscope
Aged 16. Sweating on a hot day in Dad's work van
'Who's gonna wanna look at you?',
said Dad whilst stuck in a three-mile traffic jam
Me, too nervous to take my shirt off but I wanted to be seen
To be both the driver and the passenger
Never think twice about taking my shirt off
Playing periscope, heatwave, 1997
Kissing a boyfriend, shirt off,
us only wearing shorts whilst sat back upper deck
Driver, glance up the periscope all you like
Next time, I'll kiss him in my birthday suit.

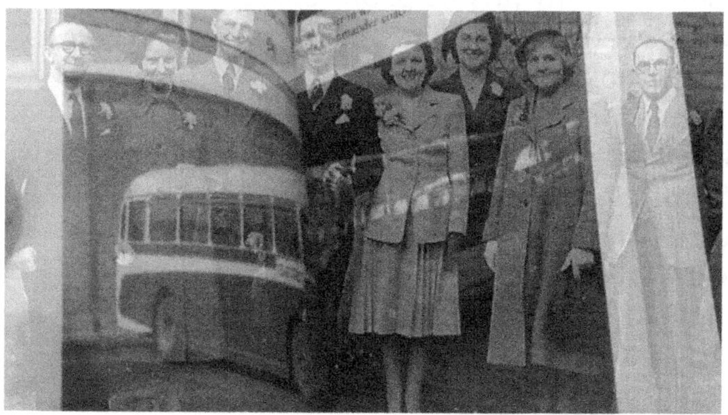

Figure 10
Still from poetry film *Periscope* by Lee Campbell (2023)
My great grandad Ronald James is standing far left.
Mum's great aunty Rose is the second lady from right standing behind Nanny Sheila who has just married grandad Ronald George circa 1950

LET RIP: TEENAGE SCRAPBOOK

My schoolteacher said I should keep a scrapbook
of images catching my attention
What happens now if I go back thirty years and look
at a time when me being me I dare not mention?
To my teacher's surprise was my scrapbook
I kept scrapping for five or so years
Homophobic eyes fuelling my shame
Heteronormative culture provoking my fears
Too often too lonely with my scrapbook and tears
Every tear, every tear in my scrapbook
Each image with its own special meaning
Images of men for girls everywhere to look
Being gay in a straight world dreaming
Ripping out bits from that week's *Smash Hits* for my scrapbook
My bedroom wall, my private public space
Then from the wall, I glued hundreds of images and lyrics
into my scrapbook
Yet all I wanted to look at was his face
But the handsome man's face was carefully placed in between
Images from *National Geographic Magazine*
I became a master of collaging those I desired
in amongst images of others and places I had been
Always liminal. Clever at seeing without being seen
The artists she taught me all turned out to be queer
Did she know something I didn't, my teacher Miss Cavalier?
Now so obviously glaring, my rip-outs of Keith Haring
And Robert Mapplethorpe's photos of men, erotic and daring
Yet, this was the time gay men were perceived
We all have AIDS many straight folks believed
Maybe that's why I didn't fully enquire
in the artists Miss taught me for fear of the fire

Look in my scrapbook, I remember his songs
But my eyes were on his chest and what's under those thongs
Jesus to a Child - such a sad song that he sung
I'll never forget George Michael all wet
In the video for *Fast Love,* all my Christmases come!
With his intellect, creativity, and eyes deep blue
My student crush at art school was another George too
That scrapbook photo of me and George on a beach
Feelings for George that I had nobody could teach
In Paris, my heart broke. Not me he was kissing
Photo of me dancing alone to Everything but the Girl's *Missing*
There came a day when I threw away
my too heavy to carry too bulky to manage scrapbook
Before I destroyed my scrapbook
I photographed all 300 pages. Lo-res, JPEG, mobile phone camera
My scrapbook now printed out as photocopies for me
to touch, to remember, to rip
as some pictures, some memories, I would rather skip.

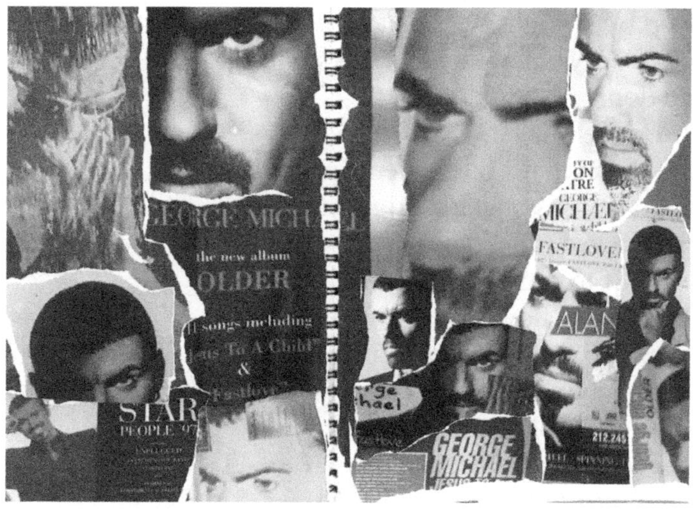

Figure 11 Pages of my teenage scrapbook circa 1996

JUICY LUCY

Juicy, juicy, Gary Lucy
Sexy bloke off *Hollyoaks*
Cheeky chappy, chappy ways
Cute eye candy, happy gays
Straight boy Gary, gay heartthrob
Got off his kit, got out his nob
On front cover, almost nude
For Nineties gay mag *Attitude*
Remember when for us gay men
now over thirty, pre the Net
When pics more dirty, hard to get
Branded bum boys, queers and benders
Gary went gay on *Eastenders*
Playing gay but gay straight-acting
I could not watch, not lost in fact in
Gary, mate, you're selling out!
Gay played by straight, what's that about?
Juicy Lucy, Gary Lucy likes it backstage,
backstage door
Gay club Heaven in 1997
I got more than what I bargained for
Three pints they say make straight men gay
Get them in bed and lead astray
'Allow myself to introduce me',
so said I to Gary Lucy
He went quiet but was not bluffing
Said it all by saying nothing
Out of Heaven, backstage door
His hotel bedroom, bedroom floor
Such a big boy Juicy Lucy
Bigger than Kriss Akabusi

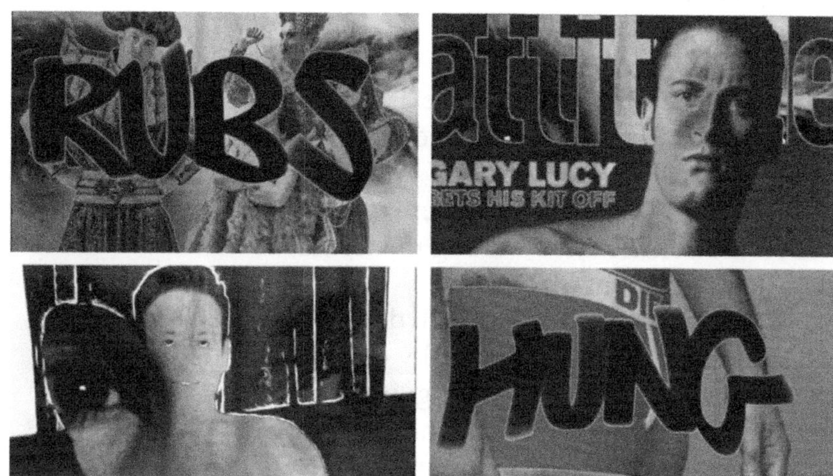

Figure 12 Stills from poetry film *Juicy Lucy* by Lee Campbell (2022)

Gary Lucy, donkey hung
like ten-mile-long Olympic run
Juicy, juicy, Gary Lucy
Cheeky bottom, cheeky ways
Let's fast forward
Where is Gary
now much older nowadays?
Gary Lucy makes a killing
acting camp as panto villain
'Out my way!' not 'Please, excuse me'
'Sign my programme Gary Lucy'
Older gay fans,
backstage door
I'm saying nothing,
nothing more
Juicy Lucy, Gary Lucy rubs our nose
in his straight camp
Stop playing Gary, you confuse me

Rub only Aladdin's lamp.

DANCING WITH SPIDERS

Get ready for action, get out of the Tube
with my cash and my condoms and plenty of lube
for Benjy's the nightclub in 2002
A dancefloor of stories, I share them with you
Right on the corner, there waiting my friend
Out of the station, out of Mile End
Pay our two quid to the man on the door
Head straight to the bar to the sticky dancefloor
Through tunnels of chrome and Egyptian sphinx
Top unbutton my shirt and spray on some Lynx
'I'm gonna get lucky, I'm gonna' me thinks
as I get to the bar and I get in the drinks
It's late Sunday nighty with Andy Almighty
His music is banging, it's half past eleven
He's playing M People's *One Night in Heaven*
He's spinning the decks as I'm downing the ciders
Men spinning their webs, we're dancing like spiders
Screw all the bullies who once called me a chunk
That one night in Benjy's, I pulled me a hunk
Got myself lucky with skater boi punk
His hair felt so sexy made spiky with gunk
We're alone in the gents now a little bit drunk
Of Givenchy Pour Homme, I liked how he stunk
Then the bulge in his jeans immediately shrunk
seeing the stains on the carpet all covered in spunk
I'm back dancing alone with my best mate Dunc
Plans of me taking punk home had in the River Lea sunk
Maybe it wasn't the carpet that caused him to run
Did he run right away seeing the hair up my bum?
True. Hardly the news to tell Dad and my Mum
London Uni rear of that year, yeah, my bottom it won!

Dad laughed and he cried, and Mum laughed, and she burst
I got a 2.1 degree, but my bum got a first!
Spinning our webs, throwing some shapes
Video screens. Videotapes
Giving it large, giving it long
to Liberty X, that week's number one song
Dunc's a part time gay. First chorus we kissed
He said it okay cos right then he was pissed
Always thought he was a beautiful opportunity missed
Took my chances 3rd chorus, he pushed me away
Looked at me dirty said, 'I'm not a gay!'
Left me there standing, I punched the air with my fist
Back on the floor and I'm losing my knees
I can't drink any more but I'm wanting some sleaze
Sniff some more poppers and take some more E's
Pissed, I'm a cub and I fancy this bear
Let's get out of this club and get home to his lair
Everything banging but then it all stops

Spiders frozen in time

Silence drops

All of us spiders wonder what's wrong
Gone everything all Pete Tong
Starting to sweat
Never forget
Memories come back
Admiral Duncan attack
Three years before
Three dead on the floor
What's going on?
Another nail bomb?

Spider to spider, 'What this about?'
Then DJ Andy yells:
'Spiders! Newsflash! Him off *Pop Idol* has come out!'

I stand thinking there of a gay Gareth Gates
He reminds me of Danny, one of my mates
Same spiky black hair and same sexy dark eyes
But Gareth I thought, well that's a surprise
But then I discovered that I had been stung
The *Pop Idol* come out was a Mr Will Young

Didn't fancy the late-night Benjy's amateur strip
So, I put on my coat, and I do up the zip
Going home on my own on the number 8,
I thought about Danny. Why is he straight?
If you fancy a straight and you are a gay,
twenty years later, here's what I have to say:
Where there's a Will, there's a Gareth
And where there's a Gareth, there's a way.

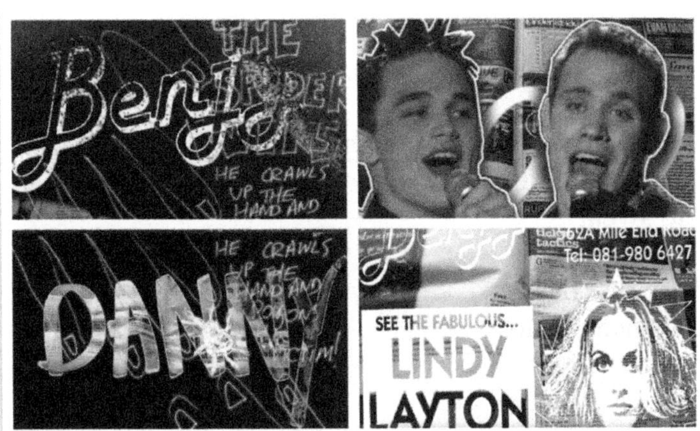

Figure 13
Stills from poetry film *Dancing with Spiders* by Lee Campbell (2023)

SATISFACTION

Getting clever at looking at men as a teen
without being seen,
I thought covert operations were all on me
I soon learnt quite the opposite in 2003
Working as a junior clerk at BJ Sales
Despite the job's boredom, I've got a scrapbook of tales

With shoulder pads so large, thinking she was in charge,
stuck-up receptionist Deb thought I was a pleb
I fancied her boyfriend in the warehouse, the skill I learnt here is:
Observing men in work overalls whilst minding my own biz

Working with Andrew and Bobby and John in their London office
Signs in gold on its walls, the words:

LEAKAGE. SATISFACTION. PROFITS

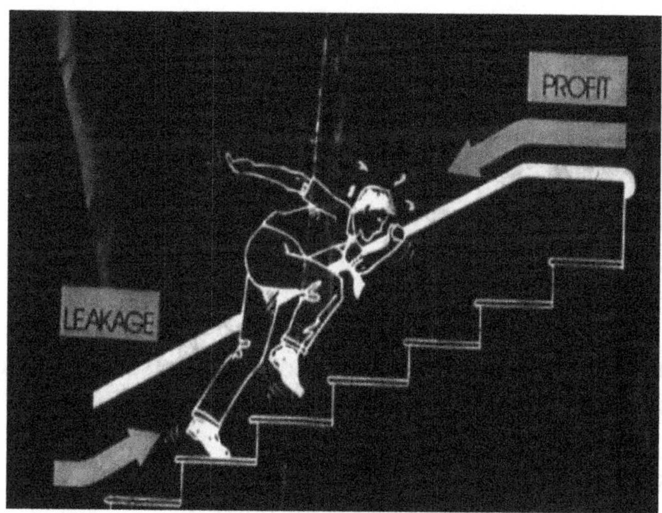

Figure 14
Still from poetry film *Satisfaction* by Lee Campbell (2020)

I shared my desk with Bobby, always sat at his computer
All day secretly browsing Gaydar to find his next male suitor
I soon learnt Bobby's own idea of the word 'satisfaction'
was how far would he go to get some action
From the time he clocked in, to the time he would go
All I could hear over our desk was,
'YOU'RE MATCHED, SAY HELLO'

Then there was Andrew, a timid man
who ate cold baked beans for his lunch straight out of a can
He had two kids and a wife but lead a double life
He couldn't wait to work late
then come a quarter to eight he was out on his date
with his muscular daddy at the Kings Arms Pub
where Andrew loved being daddy's little boy cub
Spending the hours before, on the draw
His fantasies of Daddy made alive in his pencil drawing
Hoping that as he was doodling, the manager ignoring

I remember our manager, educated at Eton
He liked to tell everyone his sales record cannot be beaten
A strait-laced fella, doing things by the book
And if your sales fell short, he'd give you one hell of a look
But Mr BJ 'Bellingham-Jones to you' was not all he seems
when I discovered he'd been having his own covert dreams
Walking into his office, without a knock,
me and Andrew left gobsmacked in utter shock
No way in the job spec for anyone's jobby,
Bellingham-Jones was getting satisfaction from salesman Bobby
And I dare not share the stories that I have about John,
just use your imagination, you won't be far wrong
The message here is in how far Bobby goes;
covert operations are right under your nose.

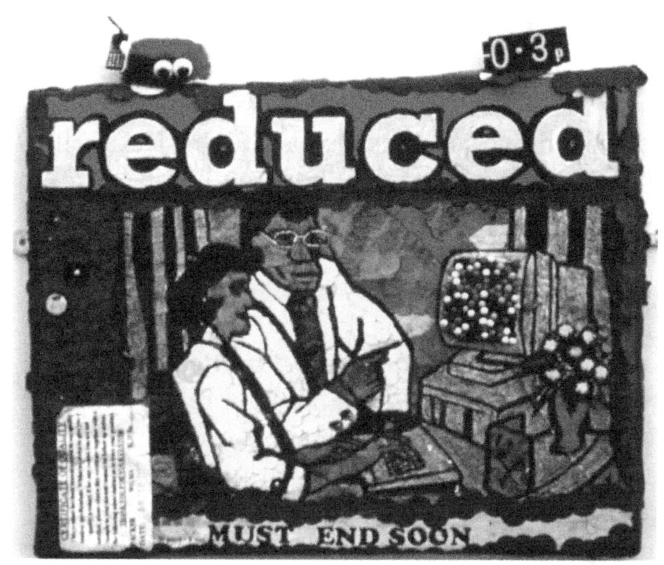

Figure 15
Reduced, mapping pins and mixed media on canvas (2000)

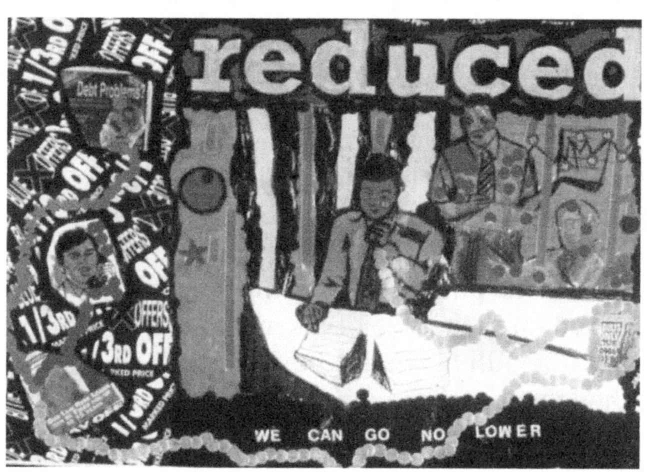

Figure 16
Reduced (We Can Go No Lower),
mapping pins and mixed media on canvas (2000)

RECLAIMING MY VOICE

A pint in my local, Christmas Day 1999
First time I looked over at Danny and thought 'Damn, he is fine'
Playing pool with the lads, Danny-boy on my mind
Bent over the table, that peachy behind
His wife on the phone saying turkey is served
I quick brushed up against him
Phwoar, his peaches were curved
Go home to your wife, to your not-so-fun life
I'll sit here with my beer and imagine your rear
You bloody enjoyed it though you said it was nothing
Be me not your wife and the turkey you're stuffing
Feeling forlorn once Danny had gone
Me back in my bedroom with Christmas pudding and porn

Danny later took me aside during a footie lads meet
And told me he knew I was gay by the way that I speak
'Don't bother me mate,' he said, 'that particular street
But I hope I don't catch it; did you get it from something you eat?
I'm not gay, I was just having a peek
at the size of Ben's tackle whilst he was having a leak
I might listen to Kylie and boogie to Chic
I got a big hard on when Ben did a streak
Running naked at the footie last week,
him running over the pitch when the Gunners got beat
All of us lads admired the size of his meat
But me, a full time full blown gayboy
Sure. I've thought about dipping my toe in but never my feet!'

Growing up with the lads
Acting my lad-self amongst my mates
Who liked women and I liked men
Still doing things that 'lads' do
But me not being straight is what differentiates
Me from them
We all drank beer and played pool in the pub
And then I opened my mouth to speak

And my voice, its tone, its hue
Its texture separates
Me from them
We do not sound the same, my voice creates
an almost immediate reaction
'You sound like that poof off the telly', the barmaid commented
I then hated the sound of my own voice
And so, I closed my mouth and did not speak

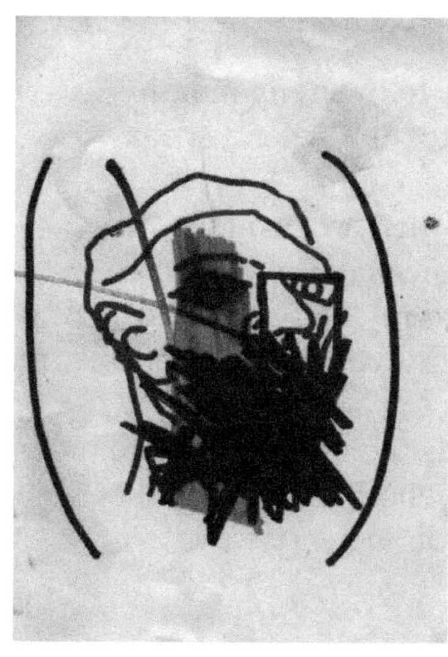

Figure 17 Felt-tip drawing (2005)

This was a time in my life
when I thought sounding camp perpetuates
negative stereotypes straights have of gays
Did my voice give away
My hidden secret I kept at bay
Trying not to divide me from them
Sound manly, act the geezer on my Harley
Hide that in my bedroom, I learnt the language of gay Polari
Be the bloke when I spoke
'Alright mate', 'Alright Dad'
I tried to sound more 'lad'
when I opened my mouth to speak

Years later someone said my voice
so evidently indicates my life
I was born with this voice. I did not have a choice
My voice no longer haunts me, it liberates
It's no longer me and them
it's we
And so now I choose to open my mouth
and take pride in its texture when I speak

We are all the same, men are just men
So, the lads like Bernice and I like Ben
I've recently liberated my body from years of self-shaming
Now it's the turn of my voice that I'm firmly reclaiming
And my mannerisms too
Move aside who finds them too camp and too gay
I'm now reclaiming who I am
This is my reclamation in every way.

CHAPTER 2: CRUISING AND BRUISING

SEE ME

1994. Me a boy no more
I needed to see men like me
Listening to my Summer 1994 mix-tape walking
through London's Gay Soho

Mix-tape boy. So much joy
Nervous yet emancipated, a space so animated
My first time in a place with men like me everywhere

Bears and cubs don't just live in the forest

How excited I was the first time a guy gave me a stare
The kind us gays know means 'I fancy you, bear'
First time in The Duke of Welly for guys like me
with a similar size belly

July 2020. I walk through London's Soho
Headphones on
Listening again to that same Summer 1994 mixtape
Retracing steps, retracing memories, retracing kisses
The first time walking around Gay Soho for many months
These streets that shaped my life appear like a dystopia
I cannot describe this elegy, this desolation
Bars and pubs now closed
Their bricks and mortar remain
but their insides are empty
Devoid of bodies. Devoid of laughter
No music can be heard. No bodies can be seen
No kisses can be felt, just remembered

I remember first kissing a guy with hairy bodily fur
Now that seems even further far gone, even more of a blur
Bodies of hair and bearded faces replaced by dead air
inside boarded-up spaces

And yet this is a strange kind of missing
The first time I felt an almost distant violent absence
I am still troubled by what that I see in my community

I remember the first time I got dirty looks
from certain bears with disapproving stares

Someone said I should emancipate from this hate
But these wounds are hard to heal
Tongue lashings cut deep
Queer space is not straightforward
Queer space is troublesome
A historied palimpsest of community unrest
troubled up from those outside and from those within

Where is 'home' now?
Where can my body just 'be'?
Where can I now perform my visibility
in physical space?
Where will we call home now?
Will I and my fellow queers who
inhabited these spaces become invisible
as our safe spaces disappear?
Will we too disappear or will something new emerge?
A new means to perform my being me, to see and be seen

An ending marks a beginning.

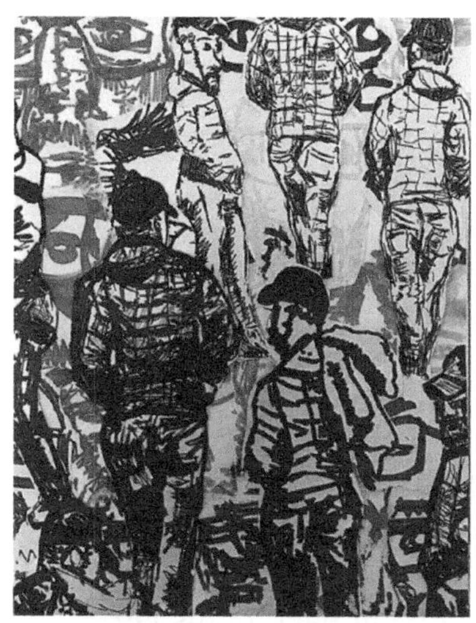

Figure 18 *Eye, I, Eye, I.* Felt-tip drawing (2020)

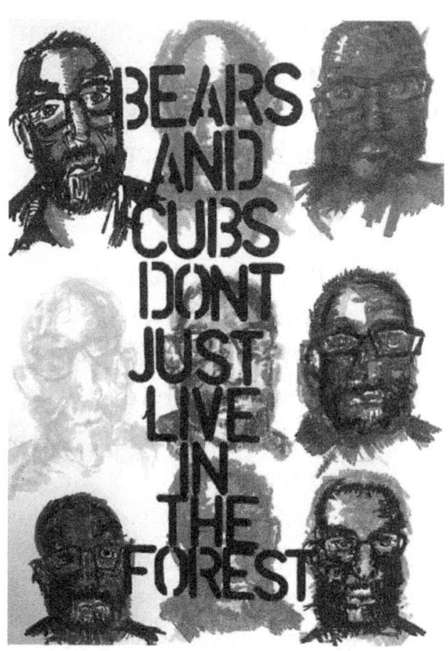

Figure 19 *Bears and Cubs Don't Just Live In The Forest* Felt-tip drawing (2020)

SPINACH AND EGGS

Early Noughties in my early twenties
Kings Arms Soho

Inside at the bar, a koala and polar
were getting it on over whisky and cola
Leather black sofa, having a gander
A cub with his paws all over a panda

Bears and cubs in their tribes
Bears over there, cubs to their sides
Getting my paw into a bear
His honey and more I want back in his lair

'A chaser', I said 'please to go with my gin'
Barman rubbing his head but then gave me a grin
'Allow me to teach you', said barman, 'I must divulge'
Pointing over to where was a bear with a bloody big bulge
It's then when I learnt what a bear chaser means
Men who like bears and the bulge in their jeans

But then I was shook from the look of an otter
His dark hairy chest was a hundred times hotter
Then turning around, opportunity knocks
I was getting the look from a wolf and a fox!
'Hey cubby,' said wolf whilst smoking a cig
'Are you a pup or are you more pig?'

Queer is a disruption. We are the disruptors
Young queer people are space architects
Imagineers creating spaces that destroy our fears
In our safe spaces we thrive and our beauty comes alive

Yet these spaces we create, we animate
by constant self-policing
Say the right thing. Body image. Include. Exclude
We're feeling quite oppressed ourselves

I could feel the woods in the stare
of this most uptight bear,
'You could do with losing a few'
but the only thing I was losing was my mind
Always two steps forward, always two steps back
Bullied at school for being gay,
now bullied by bears for being wrong fat
A community that preaches 'BE YOURSELF. Be you, but not you'
How fucked up is that!

Just when I thought I had finally caught
the eye of a rather nice guy
as I stood at the bar with my Stella Artois
He made me think he may buy me a drink
come over and ask when I was here last
and finally extinguish parts of my past
You found the matches

Your coldness pushed me back into the heat
of the fire and flames of those playground games
that names and shames
those who do not aspire
to be Mr Muscular hyphen Heteronormative
Thank you, Mr How-to-Kill-Desire

Through his Bacardi and coke and cigarette smoke,
this excuse for a bloke cracked joke after joke:
'Blue eyed boy Lee, I love your dark hairy legs
Shame the rest of your frame is like pie from Greggs

Be more like me, on spinach and eggs
You can't be a cub, you're far too old
Put those legs out on show if you want to get sold'

I'm getting quite tripped on these bodies all ripped
Imagine mine stripped and everything flipped

Mr Spinach and Eggs, stick your rules and regs
in the hole at the back of the top of my legs!

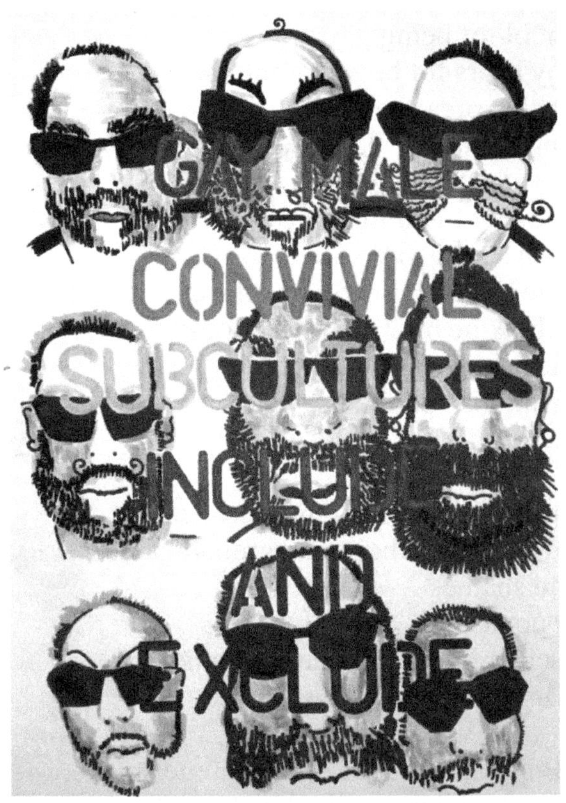

Figure 20 *Gay Male Subcultures Include and Exclude*
Felt-tip drawing (2020)

HANKY PANKY

Handkerchief on his behind, has this gay guy called Frankie
Know what's on his mind, just from the colour of his hanky
Red means only hands, he wants just winky wanky
Shower, if it's green, must clean your pinky panky
Black, the flip of that, he likes it minky manky
Blue hanky, his behind, has our guy called Frankie
He's feeling so inclined, up for some hanky panky
Brown in Chinatown, the sons of Widow Twankey
Yellow, only tall, he likes men linky lanky
Purple, only small, as short as Jimmy Krankie
Blue hanky, his behind, has our guy called Frankie
You're feeling so inclined, you're up for hanky panky
Crimson, he's got cash inside the binky banky
Hanky is orange, he'll dine you swinky swanky
Yellow, yank his chain, give it good yinkee yankee
Blue hanky, his behind, has your guy called Frankie
What's that? You're colourblind?
You thought he wearing orange hanky
If pink, put what you think inside his blankety blanky
White, get out your whip, give him good spinky spanky
Grey means okay say that he's a skinky skanky
Blue hanky, his behind, you hook up with our guy Frankie
Both feeling so inclined, both up for hanky panky
Bad luck you're colourblind. I bet your tongue won't thank me
Blue, you're rimming poo out of his stinky stanky!

DEVIL'S HOLE

One night, me aged 19 in 1997,
I was bored cruising guys in London's Heaven
So, I caught the bus, around half eleven
to this cruising spot called the Devil's Hole
My first time hiding behind this oak
Waiting nervous there for a willing bloke
Trying to get my bum out but my belt was broke
Will I get any action in the Devil's Hole?
Kneeling amongst the honeysuckle
My trousers down - I ripped the buckle
Soon enough, I'm in a puddle
As deep as the ocean in the Devil's Hole
Never did I think I would get this damp, this soaking, dripping wet
from me telling a stranger that I would let him
pee all over me in the Devil's Hole
He seemed at first such a charming fella
I wish now that I'd bought my raincoat and umbrella
His wee had the smell of around five pints of Stella
I'm drowning in the Devil's Hole
When he asked me, 'You into water sports?'
I thought, 'Yeah. Where's my goggles and swimming shorts?'
I had no idea he meant very different sorts
Piss and poo play at the Devil's Hole
Sinking, stinking, freezing, smelly
Got me thinking I'd rather be at home in front of the telly
than being pissed and shat on,
the contents of this bloke's bladder and belly
Oh, to be in the warm eating my mother's homemade
toad in the hole.

SPOKESFIST

Chariots, the now closed East End sauna,
a place of seeing and being seen
Glances then between gay men
through the clouds of mist and steam
How can you forget the bubbles floating in the sauna jacuzzi?
Didn't care who sucked you off in there,
underwater we weren't choosey
Where to go to see men, in the jacuzzi where we lay
Bathing in the bubbles of other bloke's semen
at Chariots back in the day
With a name as grand as Chariots, one expected at their selection
Bodies of Classical Greek proportions,
Renaissance Michelangelo perfection
But there were no Greek gods here, just flabby middle-aged queens
being sucked off by teenage chavs and twinks
or at least they were in their dreams
Cubs and otters and foxes, koalas, pigs and bears
Wolves and pups and pandas, lounging over sauna chairs
What animal you chose to call yourself
or what others they called you,
most called *Chariots* a sauna, well I called it a zoo

High on heat and poppers, this hairy cub, I couldn't resist
And before I knew, I was in his poo, up his bum I shoved my fist
Didn't know back then, it was a fetish,
putting your fist inside a man
My body came over all peckish I swear,
I had no control over my hand
Oh, if only my body could talk, oh if only my fist could speak
Mr Hand, can you help me understand, what's it like
going up inside another man's street?

LEE'S FIST SPEAKING:

'Well, it was certainly a new experience Lee,
I sure could tell some tales
On the bus, on the way back home Lee,
I remember you cleaning his shit out of my nails
It's surprising what gets stuck in there, I felt all manner of things
A swallowed silver sixpenny piece
and a couple of engagement rings
Though nice and warm up inside him, please just before you shove
me up another man's arsehole in the future,
put on me a rubber glove
Lee, HSBC in 2006, at its Canary Wharf HQ
Well, I was expecting then to get up some banker's bum
and feel what it's like, financial poo
You taught English to their foreign workers,
'I'm going international now!', I thought
And you used to creep into their top floor member's gym
without ever getting caught
That first time you went into the sauna,
I thought, 'This is my lucky day!
Soon I'll be up inside a German's arse,
they're well tight so they say
You're going to have to work extra hard now Lee, they're straight,
these banker boys. Bet they've never thought about me
in their range of sexual pleasure toys'
But you just sat there watching them sweating over coals
And there was me ready to go, get up inside their holes!
Hand cream on, just had manicure, nails filed and perfectly smooth
I was ready to go on a worldwide tour and get back in the groove

When you just sat there happily watching them,
maybe for you that were enough
seeing these metrosexual men trying to act all tough?
Were you thinking on your feet then Lee?
I guessed that's how it goes
Had you replaced me with your foot then Lee,
were you fisting with your toes?
Just don't forget all the times I was laughed at
by your heterosexual mates
Because I didn't give a firm grip
when they pulled out their hands for shakes
In the sauna, I thought this was my chance
to make them understand
Make them think twice before they ask all nice,
'Hey Lee, do you mind giving me a hand?''

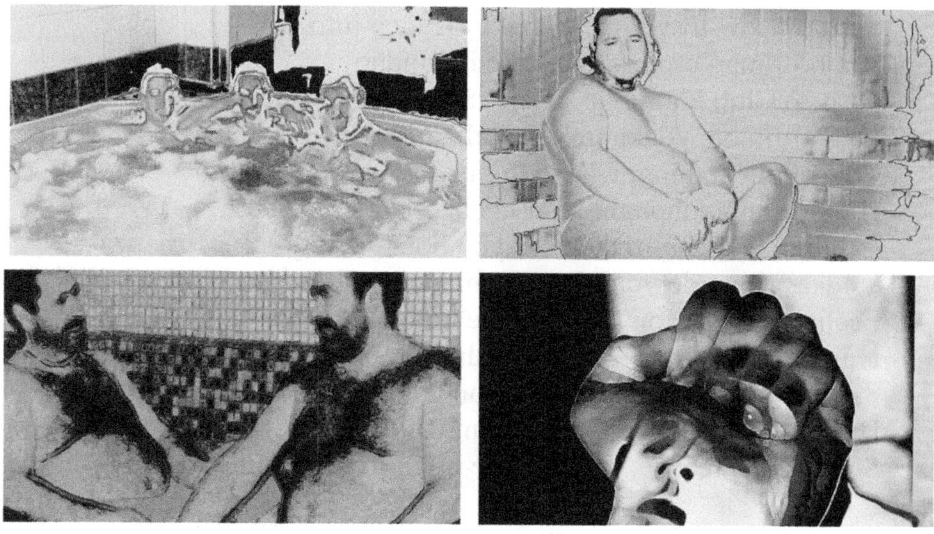

Figure 21
Stills from poetry film *Spokesfist* by Lee Campbell (2023)

HIMBO JIMBO

Himbo himbo, do you know the lingo?
Gay man slang for gay male bimbo
Himbo himbo, have you got the lingo?
His name's James but he's 'Himbo Jimbo'
Himbo Jimbo, whilst he's reading Rimbaud
trying to look smart with his legs apart akimbo
Himbo Jimbo, so you're not in limbo
Shiny decorations looking shit just after Chrimbo
Himbo Jimbo, name's got quite a ringo
Says he's wearing Dior
but sure, that's end of sale bling though
Himbo Jimbo, got to feel for him though
Mum is on the run, his Dad's a Tory jingo
Himbo Jimbo's sweet chariot can swing low
See how low it swings, is that too much info?
Himbo Jimbo on that app called Grindbo
Goes to Club Flamingo where the gay male vermin go
Himbo Jimbo, vodka mixed with Vimto
Thing quite a thing, what a thing you had for him bro
Himbo Jimbo, thought your chances slim though
Pull him in the gym then bar you both go in go
Vodka Vimto down in Bar Domingo
Feeling rather happy like you're winning on the bingo
Himbo Jimbo, through your bedroom window
Says he likes it dirty, better clean around the rim though
Himbo Jimbo, now you've learnt the lingo
Soon you'll realise, he's got the brain of half a gingo!

THE TALE OF BENNY HARRIS

Come closer dears to best aunt nell
A bar in London's Dilly, so begins my tale
where days gone by a Lilly raid
gave danger and thrills to omees seeking trade

Frequented by fruit of a certain age
whose once zhooshy décor is now well past fade
In Bar Fabulousa, it was anything but
made famous wide over for the local slut
I'm surprised the Hilda Handcufffs did not have it shut
for how a certain dilly boy Benny liked to strut

Dears around the bar from afar ajax
Dressed in frocks and high sling-backs
Their expensive smellies could not hide the facts
that this was Dilly's most prime of all its meat-racks

This feely omi walks in, and before you ask it
You could see through his cats his bona basket
Amongst the antique HP's was one besotted fungus
who rather admired dilly boy's corybungus
Mincing around like a model in Paris
He gave him the name, Benny Harris
A nice arse on a guy, as not to embarrass
In Polari slang, we say he's got a 'bene aris'

'Filly dilly' says Fungus, 'hello, boyno.
I won't be strange, I'm alamo
I know a brandy latch near here where we can go
Don't get me wrong I'm no size queen
But this schvartza's cheap, just ten quartereen'
Sadly, for Fungus, a ferricadooza

Benny's yews were on the thews of another cruiser
Benny's excitement soon ended in scharda
when the barman took him aside and told him to nellyarda
'Benny, mais oui, that number is nice to vada
But take it from me, Andy only tips the brandy
rather than charver an aspro-arva
Have a shot of Vera. You'll vada things clearer
She's part time in the life, got chavvy and wife
Not full time so, she parkers the measures
to feel what it's like to have omee pleasures
Look she's on the polari pipe now dear, nelly her mutter
Her taxi driver back home is her pastry cutter'

Benny starts writing Andy a billy doo
When all of sudden, screams of
'BETTY BRACELETS! GARDY LOO!'
A charpering omee walks in and goes over to Ben
Benny worried he'll get arrested and locked up in queer ken
The omee whispers into one of Benny's polari lobes,
'You dare not repeat this. Nanti panarly
I think your bona vardering
Meet me out back in ten minutes by my Harley'

Benny's rogering cheat is overflowing letch water
as he's putting on the dish up this orderly daughter
Lilly turns round on his back onto his Jim and Jack
Sniffing purple hearts sees first time Benny's cartes
Lilly omee shouts: 'YOUR NADA TO VADA IN THE LARDER!',
leading to one fatal palaver
'You promised more carnish up my dish
You're getting no gent, you lying rent'
Benny schonks him on his onk as Lilly tries to scarper
Then Benny doing his right, turns the murderous arva

In front of the beak in the court of law
Benny retells all he saw,

'I thought it was my heart he was out to shush
but all he wanted was my cartes up his tush'
Whilst in queer ken, Benny had the odd blag
But soon became known as the singing lag
finding fame as a number climbing the slanging tree
Benny became quite the star, believe you me
Did the other lags think his Polari songs were naff
Or could they see his talent in crafting songs so vaf
Singing 'Who cares if your cartes is on the tad bijou
It's not the top insides of your strides
that makes you bonaroo'
Bet it came as a surprise,
lags singing about the colour of their eyes
Well, that's all my dears. Amen, larlou!

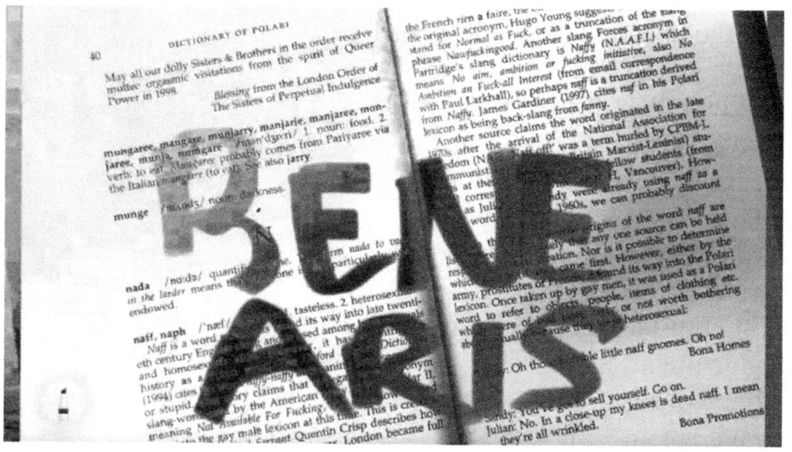

Figure 22
Still from poetry film *The Tale of Benny Harris* by Lee Campbell (2023)

STD

You gave me an STD
So said the nurse in the pharmacy
You gave me an STD
Her proctoscope up inside of me
You gave me an STD
Sitting on the throne like His Majesty
You gave me an STD
So said the bloke on the BBC
You gave me an STD
Sitting on your throne on your lavatory
You gave me an STD
Sitting out the back on your balcony
You gave me an STD
So said the nun reading NME
You gave me an STD
Like the vicar's son done for perjury
You gave me an STD
So said the app from the Doc's for free
You gave me an STD
App told me that in the cemetery
You gave me an STD
Now I'm in the shit with my family
You gave me an STD
Feel it in my shit up my cavity
You gave me an STD
Drinking out your cup, same cup of tea
You gave me an STD
Now the word 'poof' in my poo and pee
You gave me an STD
I'm not gay, straight as can be
You gave me an ST … hang on,
when we had sex mate, didn't we use a pack of three?

USED TO BE

Used to be slim, used to be trim
Used to get 'Wouldn't mind getting with him!'
Used to be star in the gay bar
Used to get 'Ooh, how handsome you are'
Used to take mates out on some dates
Bar taken now over by straights
Used to be fit, workout a bit
Used to get 'Look at the bottom on it!'
Used to be young, used to be hung
Used to climb up top of the rung
Used to get pulled, used to get called
names which now I feel appalled
Used to dance beat. Sat in their seat,
older gay men calling us 'meat'
We were just toys over the noise
West End Girls, Pet Shop Boys
Used to be twink, used to half think
they just saw me, bit of young mink
Used to wear two white Jimmy Choo
Tight cotton fit, camouflage poo
Used to wear double over my bubble
Men and their shit, nothing but trouble
Back of Top Shop used to quick swap
Poo on my Choo. Chew on my chop
Never thought bad, used to be glad
attention I had, me scantily clad
Used to shave hair, head and elsewhere
All over smooth, now I prefer bear
Used to be slim, used to be trim
Used to get 'Wouldn't mind getting with him!'
Yeah, I was svelte yet always felt
not a kind hand, cards I'd been dealt

Used to let men over again
make me feel I was one out of ten
Yeah, I got pulled though names I got called
made me feel like from under a rock, I had just crawled
Used to eyes lock with jock after jock
In it for love, of course they were not
Used to think of all the above
Never thought I worthy of love
Used to get pissed, touched up and kissed
More than a shag not on his list
Used to regret odd guy I met
More than just fun in the toilet
Pushed them away. Used to I'd say
'Only for play, end of the day'
Used to think charm was there in my palm
Shooting his drugs up through his arm
Used to act dumb and uncomfortably numb
Seeing him shoot drugs up his bum
Used to think norm, come early morn
Me still asleep, the other guy gone
Used to buy clothes from Top Man I goes
Then I saw size, that's when I froze
Triple XL. Got on the scale
Thought 'Bloody hell, size of a whale!'
Then I gym hard. Then I swim hard
Six times a week membership card
Used to think 'Shit! Putting on a bit!
How much fat in this one chip?'
Used to count cals. Went off the rails
Down in the deep, dietary hells
Used to obsess. Never undress
Don't serve me Eton mess
Used to watch weight. Got in a state
Two lettuce leaves, dinner on plate

Used to be slim, used to be trim
Used to get 'Wouldn't mind getting with him!'
Knocking on wood. Used to look good
but never loved me, way that I should
Boy, I've come far since the gay bar
Don't need a man to know who you are
Used to pull men over again
But this is me now, that was me then
Used to ride tubes cruising for dudes
Now all they see is belly and boobs
Now not as fit, getting on a bit
Now I get 'Look at the belly on it'
Now not as slim, now not as trim
Now I get 'Better get back in the gym'
Now not so young. Now I'm half hung
with these man boobs bigger than Mum
Who cares I'm not svelte? Happiest felt
Give me more cheese, please on my melt
Me and my bro meant to stay low
Meant to stay hid. Never on show
We were once young. Now getting stung
Muscle Marys, malicious with tongue
Dare if we did open the lid
Muscle Marys, want us all rid
Think men our age should get off the stage
Never go out. Stay in our cage
Used to be slim, used to be trim
Used to get 'Wouldn't mind getting with him!'
Used to be twink, now I just think,
'LOOK IN THE MIRROR, MUSCLE MARY IN PINK!'

THE RECKLESS HOMOSEXUAL

For the unreciprocated,
the obsessive,
the infatuated,
and the envious,
a late-night lament for the reckless homosexual

Only in the calm of the night
and the quiet of an alone bed
at midnight, can I write this
only now, twenty years on

Only under flickering screen
in the cold light of night,
with memories for company,
now I see it, plain as day

Infatuation, quite possibly
Envy, almost certain
Bordering on obsession
Love, definitely not
Unreciprocated on your part
Knowing I was into you, you made me, and how you loved it,
reckless for you

I was a rollercoaster train going off the rails
Every text message you sent me
Heart faster beating
Screen flickering wildly
Pulse racing like a Ferrari
Narrowly missing, avoiding a crash

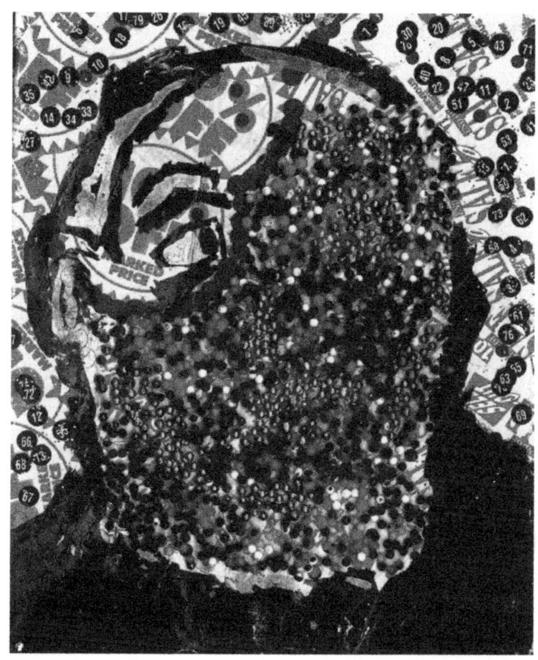

Figure 23 *Eye Spy*, mapping pins and mixed media on canvas (2005)

Two hundred mapping pins,
I stuck onto canvas
to make a portrait of you
Part homage, part artwork, part voodoo

If only someone would have hit me
hard in the face with a hammer
to shock me out of what I had become
Hammer's force so hard that I would not have felt a thing
seeing your arms wrapped around another man
As you kiss him, you look at me
sat with a date on the black sofa
Tattoos of stars on his arms
He asked nothing of me

If only he had punched me
and given me
a black eye
Maybe then I would have seen you
for what you really were
Allow him to love me
Not push him away

I awake at dawn
I read over these midnight musings
I conclude that I have written,
in the cold light of day,
a (surprisingly) careful and considered lament
on the account of me being
a former reckless homosexual.

HOT MESS

You made me feel I had to hide everything about myself
when I was much younger whilst I fancied
the hell out of you straight man

Tonight, I bumped into you on way to queer poetry night
That second, I became hot mess

Pulled on strings of your backpack to stop you and say, ‘Hi’
Quick hug as you ran for train or were you running away from me?

Even now, in just twenty seconds, you pulled my strings
I could almost hear the symphony pounding out my heart.

LUCKY DRAGON SHIRT

'If you must', us teachers told, 'do it appropriately'
You from Japan. English language lessons
Sitting shy at back of my class
Gentle Japanese man. Summer-intensive class,
you bought calm. Learning English to
study Violin at Royal College London
That moment seeing you smile at my lucky dragon shirt
Blue cotton shirt with three dragons
Number three is my lucky number
I wore shirt outside of class on the pull
Not sure why but asked you out for drink
Appropriately, of course
Chinatown upstairs boozer. 'Keep it professional', us teachers told
Sat in sofa, both our shirts inappropriately buttoned up,
mine intentionally so. Unbuttoned glimpses of your soft black
hair on chest. Not your teacher. Not my student
Feeling lucky as I bought drinks
Count to three, tell you what's on my mind
Count to three, close my eyes, kiss your cheek
Professionally, of course
'I've a girlfriend waiting for me back in Japan',
you said assertively. Maybe you did I bought it
You knew that I knew there was no girlfriend
Appropriately, of course, I knew you wanted me
in your flat in South Kensington
Five years later, you made it
Hit the big time, bestselling classical L.P
I bought it. Girlfriend or not, on every play,
dragon shirt off, lucky indeed,
you and me both having fun.
Professionally, of course.

CHAPTER 3: SEEN AND FOUND

NICE CUP OF TEA

I could see him through the drizzle
'This is the man you are going to marry,
you mark my words', whispered into one of my ears

'Oh, I remember when you two first met,
when you first met Alex', said another friend
only recently,
'You two sitting on the swings, gently swinging,
gazing into each other's eyes'

The rain came down as we first kissed
in the middle of the football field
But then made way for a clear sky sunset
as we later kissed on the Thames Path near The Angel
Could I quite believe that I had found mine?
'Did you see the smile on his face?'
said a friend when Alex said goodbye 'How happy was he'
'Yes', happy me replied
Alex's smile kept me smiling the rest of the night
and all the way into the following morning
as I got the 453 for our first date
Packed onto the bus like sardines
Sweat not just from the heat but from my anticipation
in seeing him again

And there he was just before midday as planned
sitting in Little Italy Café just off Leicester Square
smoking a cigarette and drinking a cup of tea

New memories about to be made
in spaces so familiar and historied to me
Now reconfigured and reimagined through cups of tea

First to The Poetry Café on Betterton Street
for a nice cup of tea
Then to Foyles Café on Charing Cross Road
for another cup of tea
Walking down The Mall holding each other's hand
Our first photo of us together on the grass in Green Park

Then to The Retro Bar, George Court off The Strand
for a final cup of tea
Sitting together in the black two-seater sofa
in the late afternoon as a welcome cool breeze
came through the open front door

Felt strange being here not chatting up some bloke
Eyeing up talent whilst out for a smoke
Bet the barman thought I was having a joke
when I asked for tea not my usual whiskey and coke
Me stone cold sober not passed out on the floor
Were those days now over and a new me in store?
The barman remarked,
'He's a keeper, you'll see'
Did he have foresight? Had he read the leaves in our tea?
He must have been psychic in the forces greater
as I'm now engaged to Alex my sidekick eleven years later

The bar was half empty but for me was full of memories
as the bar I had been too many times drunk in
disco danced in
smoked roll-ups in
had my heartbroken three or more times in

Had a date where the guy spent most of the time talking
about washing powder in
and where another guy with tattoos of stars on his arms
was the one who had got away in
as I could not see what was in front in me
This bar that I self-reflected in
in amongst the jukebox playing New Order
and fairy lights wrapped around the portraits of
pop stars spread across the walls like a salon of the electro-pop elite

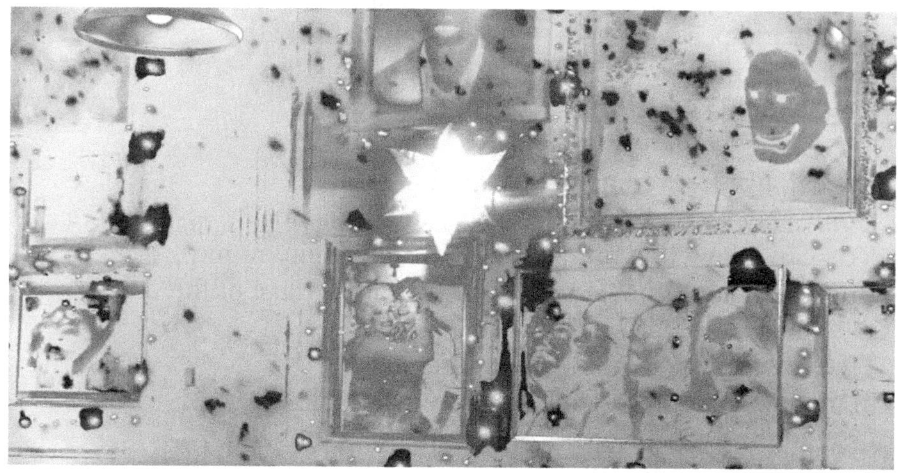

Figure 24
Still from poetry film *Nice Cup of Tea* by Lee Campbell (2022)

And now, here I was in the bar again
The smoky haze
of past drunken nights and morning after hungover days
replaced by an indescribable feeling of self-peace
just by being with Alex sitting in the pub
sharing a nice cup of tea.

RUFUS

Alex loves Rufus, a Welsh springer spaniel
I'm frightened of dogs and in need of a manual
I've often drawn Rufus to understand better
but I don't share the bond that those two have together
You might think I'm silly and I'm being pedantic
But sharing bed sheets with Rufus is far from romantic
Bubbles, bubbles, doggy troubles
Rufus all soaking. I am not having a laugh
It's my jumper Alex uses to dry him after his bath
He knows me too well when he's licking his lips
I'm under his spell when I give him my chips

Be jealousy free, come out of the fog
Don't play second fiddle when it comes to a dog
You can joke with your partner, 'It's the doggy or me!'
But when they stumble to answer, it's a marriage of three

Two weeks ago, I enter a fancy-dress shop
in my black Adidas trainers and green hoodie top
I say to the assistant that I'm looking for a dog-suit
that will fully camouflage me
'Why certainly sir, what size?' she replies
I answer, 'Oh size extra-large me'
She shows me the full range of their man size dog-suit selection
'Only Welsh springer spaniel' I say in my quest for perfection
'Here is a picture. I need an exact copy
Big brown puppy dog eyes please and ears furry and floppy'
'You are in luck' says the assistant, 'One in stock just for you.
Only two hundred pounds credit card or PayPal will do
No tumble drying allowed. Hand wash at 30 degrees
If the tail fails to wag properly, give this button a squeeze'

What if the zip on the back breaks, me getting hotter and hotter?
I'd be deep fat fried from inside my dog suit like brie or ricotta!
Stripped to my pants, I slip inside and zip up
But not before too long, I'm getting hot from being inside this pup
Not much ventilation inside this rather snug fit
Just a hole where his nose goes and where his eyes are a slit
Lesson One: Dog position, walk around on all fours
Lesson Two: Play with tennis ball not with hands but with paws
Having completed this training, I make my way to the park
I feel a great sense of achievement when I gave my first bark
'Oh, Mummy can I stroke him?', this child persistently begs
If he tries, I'll poke him. Poo up his legs
I steal the boy's ice cream, he starts shouting 'OI, YOU!'
I find a hole in my dog suit and pee all over his shoe
Back home, out my costume, my dog-self back in its box
I hide it deep in my drawer underneath all my socks
Later Alex comes home. Asks me what kind of day I have had
I reply like I do always, 'Oh the usual, not bad'

Sure, role play in dog suits is a whole kind of weird
Me dressing up as Rufus – Rufus with beard!
But I would never say to Alex, 'It's Rufus or Lee'
At the end of the day, I'm happy. Me, Alex and Rufus
and a nice cup of tea.

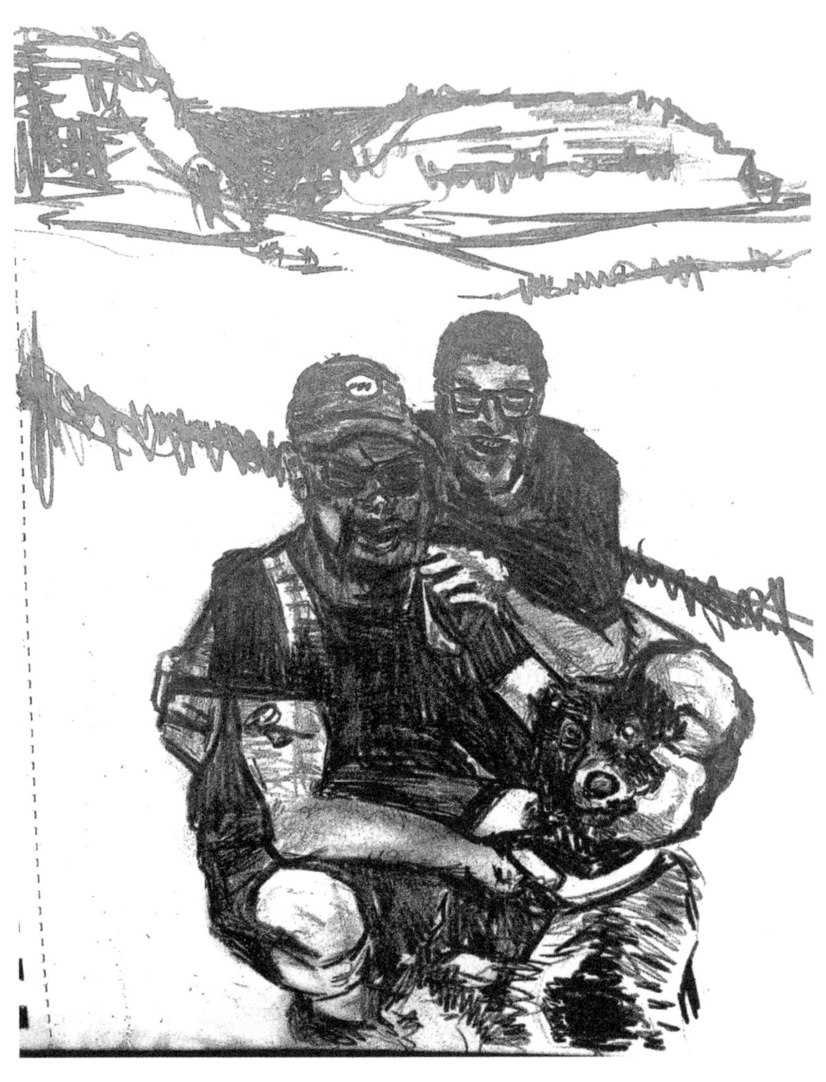

Figure 25
Lee, Alex and Rufus, pencil drawing (2019)

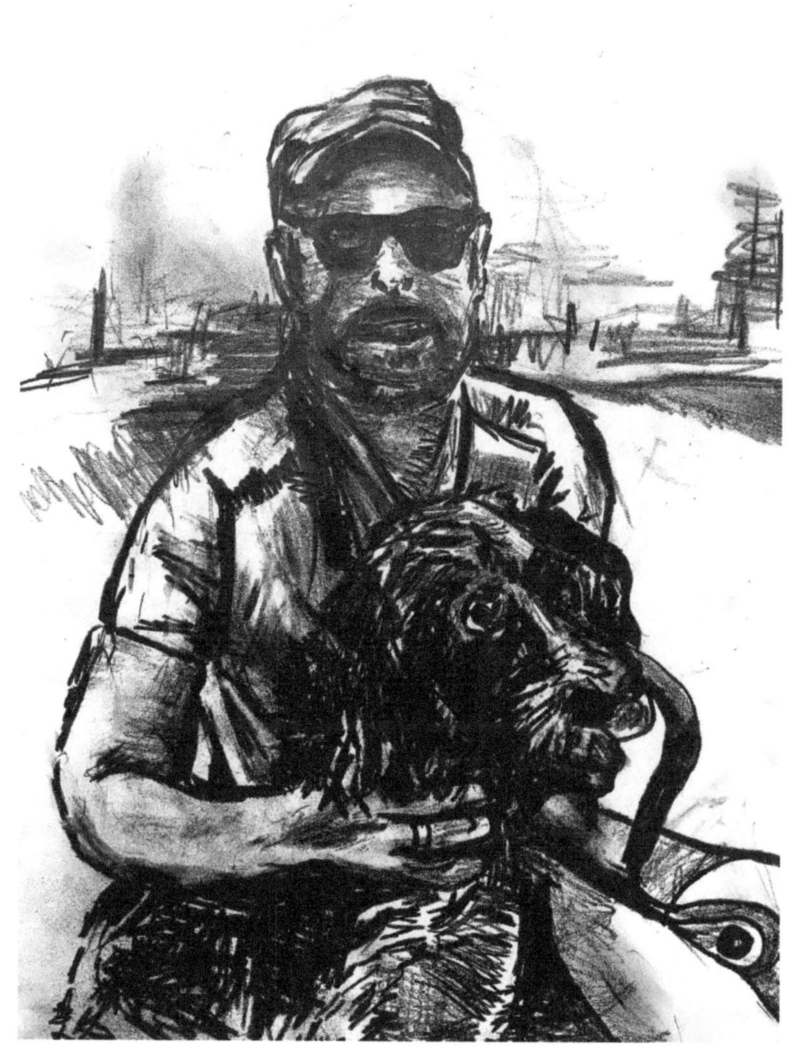

Figure 26
Alex and Rufus, pencil drawing (2019)

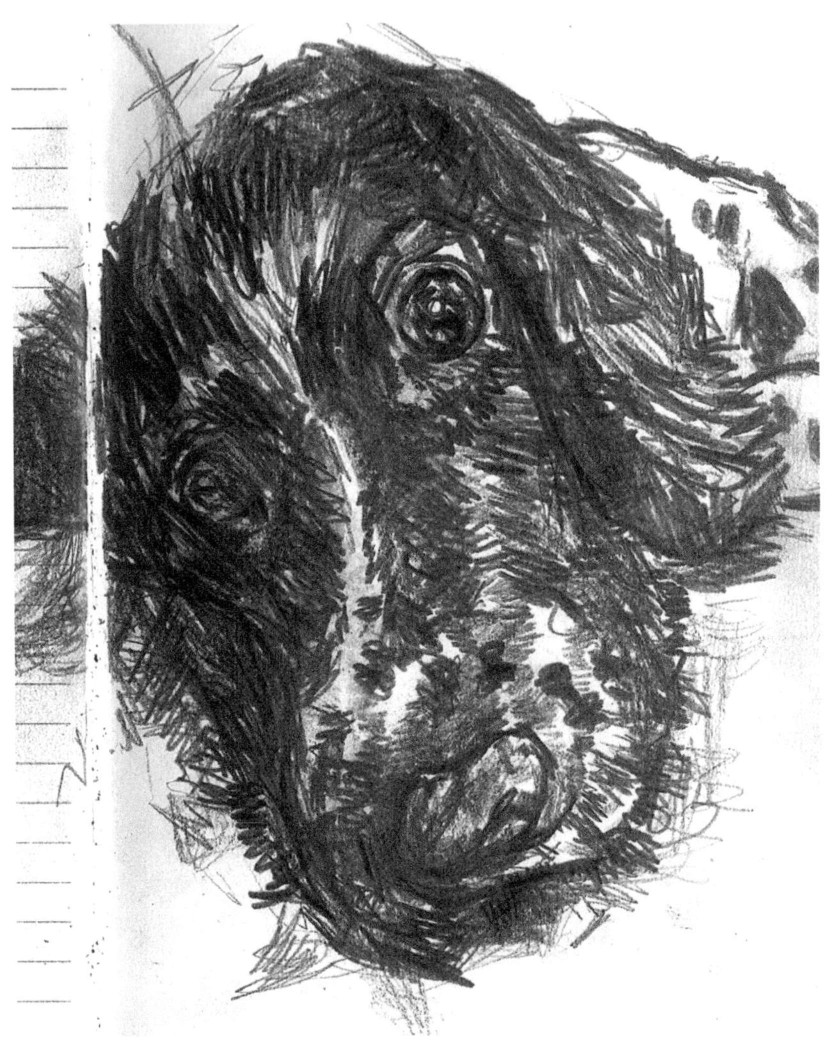

Figure 27
Rufus, Pencil drawing (2024)

BEAST

There's a beast in me, it's lurking
It don't make any sense
He comes out when I least expect it
He's watching through the fence
The beast brings out this side of me
that likes to cause offence
I tried to beat him out of me
but the beast is too intense

There's a beast in me, he's lurking
His beat is so immense
Tried hard to make amends with him
but cannot recompense
There's a beast in me, it's lurking
I like he don't make sense
When I think I've put his beats to bed,
nah, the beast is present tense.

A DOGGY WHODUNNIT

What if I dressed up as Rufus complete with dog collar?
And speak doggy voice and star in a horror?
Everyone to the slaughter, beware of his paws
Deep in the water, Rufus is Jaws

Less *Midsomer Murders*, more Hitchcock thriller
Who controls who and who is the killer?
Is it all fiction this whodunnit of mine?
Or is there some truth in who does the crime?
He's got murder in mind – just look at those eyes
They might be all sweetness, but they're sugar and lies
Delicious, delicious doggy delicious
Sweet baby Rufus can sometimes be vicious

He's one of the family, he's man's best friend
But in the dark of his kennel, he's plotting your end
This might sound dramatic. Can this get any absurder?
But that bone that you give him is a weapon of murder
Not death by the ways you've read in crime fiction
But the kind the most gruesome, by doggy infliction

The public are advised to stay well clear
of a dog wanted in connection with a murder last year
His name is Rufus and has gone on the run
He's aged seven in dog years and height 2 ft.1
He wears a brown coat with patches of grey
Have you seen Rufus? Call 999 right away

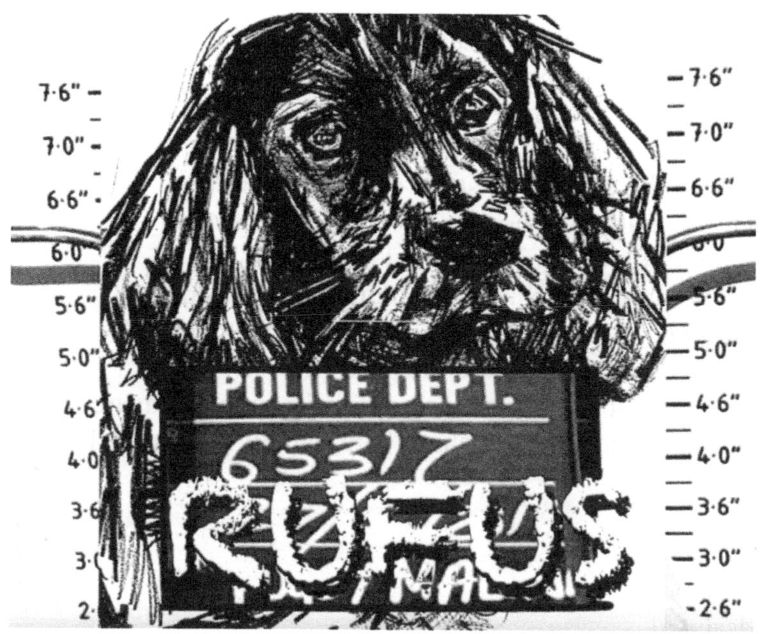

Figure 28 *Rufus, Most Wanted*
Still from poetry film *The Adventures of Rufus* by Lee Campbell (2024)

11:01 PM. On CCTV, a car was caught speeding down the A23
A witness told police, although seen from afar,
they spotted a dog at the wheel of the car
11:56 PM. In a sleepy cul-de-sac
He parks outside 16 and sneaks round the back
12:04 AM. Barking and screaming
'That's Rufus with a gun!' claims a neighbour
'But I could've been dreaming
Suddenly, in the dead of night
Screams of "Rufus, have mercy!" gave me one hell of a fright
With my torch and my golf-club, I entered next door
shivering with terror from the full horror in store

Overcome by the sting of that sinking feeling
when you see someone's blood dripping down
from the up above ceiling

Upstairs, in the bathroom, stone cold in the shower
Lay a body in its final hour
Drowning in blood, in its own red liquor
Who could do such a thing, who could get any sicker?
It's clear who's the killer just look on the floor
Trace of brown dog hair and the print of a paw
A dog is not just for Christmas but for life is the measure
He's getting life for sure, behind bars - at His Majesty's Pleasure'

R for revenge
U for unkind
F for fanatic
U underlined
S is the sentence Rufus has started
serving for murdering the dearly departed
Those capital letters together - what do you get?
R. U. F. U. S spells Rufus!
Are your palms starting to sweat?

HOW TO DRAW RUFUS

Dear Rufus,

Da Vinci drew the body to help him understand
I too have learnt about you using pencils in my hand
Four years since I first drew you
Many lessons been learned
Drawing helps overcome my dog fear
The tables have turned
It's okay Rufus, you can have them, you can take all my chips
And my pizza, take it all, can I get you some dips?
Take my jumper when its freezing, I promise not to quiver
Don't worry, for you my little dog friend, go ahead, let me shiver
I'm sorry, beg my pardon, I won't complain at your poo
Poo in my garden, its smell reminds me of you
When I wake up in the morning, and you've done a little wee
All over my expensive carpet, it will be a sight I like to see
Leave your hair on my new sofa, I won't wash it out for days
Finding hair all the way over, I don't care how long it stays
At my Christmas dinner table, guests hungry for food
Jump up and eat all the turkey
I won't shout out something rude
Remember, my little dog love, however difficult this sounds
You still can't jump up onto our bed in the middle of the night
Wake me up, lick me all over
Lie down between me and Alex
Go to sleep and snore, my little dog muse
Our bed is strictly out of bounds

Lee

P.S
Remember Rufus
When the world throws me a curve ball,
you're my trusted loyal friend
Always there to reassure me
Providing comfort in the end
Beneath the surface of my poems
lying underneath the joke
There's love in every drawing
in every line in every stroke

How do I draw Rufus?
A question many folk ask
Is it a labour of love or a gentle Sunday afternoon task?
How do I capture his dark puppy dog eyes
What's the secret? Well folks, there's no big surprise
19 pencils, and rubber, and sharpener will do
Some sheer perseverance and a beer maybe two

19 pencils, one for each graphite hardness degree
Let's start off with 14, 12, and 10 and not forgetting 8B
14 and 12 for his dark coat and wet soggy nose
For his big puppy dog eyes, 10B and 8B I chose
They are the trickiest part of Rufus to draw
But you will know when you've drawn them correctly
You will when for sure
When they stare back at you and at only that stage
will they follow you around, magically leap off the page
To draw his head at an angle, just shy of 18 degrees
Use a protractor and employ those 6, 5 and 4Bs
His eyes, if drawn correctly will command you part with your food
Rufus wants all your chips, whether they're whole or part chewed

Be strong fellow draughtsmen, he will take and will take
Don't let anyone catch you feeding him
It's a drawing for God's sake!

But feeding a drawing if Rufus is properly portrayed
is a mistake unavoidable, so easily made
For his spotty dog coat requiring medium shading
3B and B good for blending and fading
After a night asleep on his blanket, 2B for small deposits of poo
HB for stain wee or a shade lighter will do
Now we come to the H range in our instruments of lead
F, H, 2H, 3H are ideal for that quiff of hair on top of his head
Lastly 4H, 5H, and 6H for hairs of his belly
It's where he likes the most tickles but can be a bit smelly

So, there you have it, how to draw Rufus, a step-by-step guide
Follow my instructions and there will be Rufus almost in flesh
by your side

P.S
Yes, you might want to draw him in photo realist perfection
But I draw what he makes me feel inside, in my gut,
that intimate connection
Tension in lines, ripped and torn
Embody our play fights where battle lines drawn
And it is the P.S, the post-scriptum, fellow draughtsmen
that can often outweigh
Everything wrote before it, it holds what we mean to say

'Spare a thought for your dear Mum and my poor old legs
Isn't it shocking how much Sainsbury's
have put up the price of their eggs!

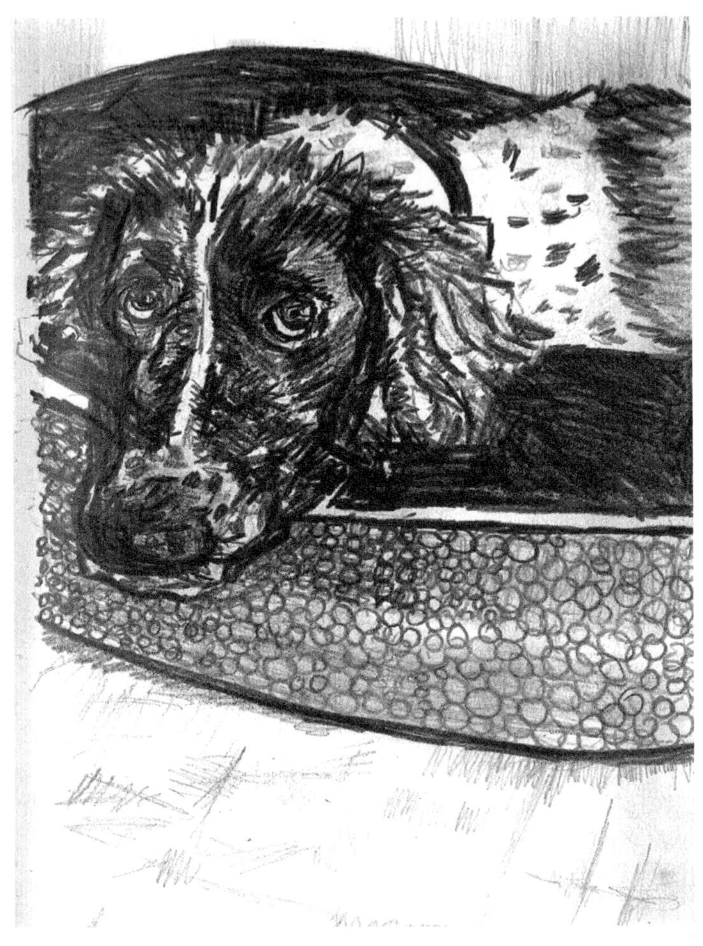

Figure 29
Rufus, pencil drawing (2023)

P.S.
Lee, I love how you have captured Rufus's deep pensive look
That one in his basket. Must have taken you ages to draw him.
Was it a couple of hours you took?'

Half reading that message on Facebook
that my mum, last November, sent to me,
I never imagined how important that post scriptum would be
When Mum passed away only a couple of days after,
who knew a post scriptum could contain
as much sadness as laughter?

If there is one thing, I hope that this poem has taught
is that the often-lowly footnote, or raft of sudden side thought
as embodied in the post-scriptum, can often hold the most weight
Be confident, say it now, not the end,
before it's too late

And so …

Dear Rufus,

When the world throws me a curve ball,
you're my trusted loyal friend
Always there to reassure me
Providing comfort in the end
Beneath the surface of my poems
lying underneath the joke
There's love in every drawing
in every line in every stroke

Lee.

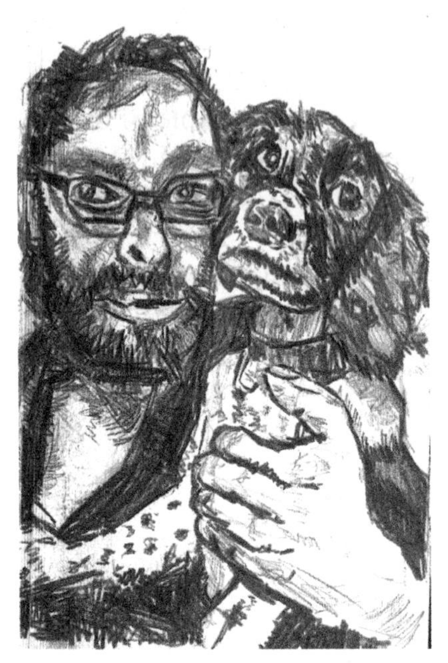

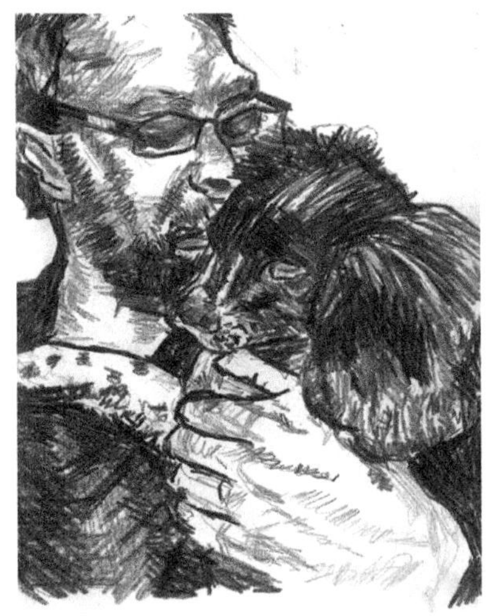

Figures 30 (top) and 31 (bottom)
Alex and Rufus, pencil drawing (2023)

THE BIG REVEAL

Wearing new trainers, and I tread in his shit
I should always remember, we only dog sit
Rufus is not actually our dog,
me and Alex have him on loan
Rufus is Alex's manager's dog
What if we had a dog of our own?

Rufus comes a few hours sometimes a few days
His hair over our sofa when overnight stays
Returns back to his normal well-behaved self
when owners collect him - Patty and Ralf

Rufus gone home, clean where he's pooed
Flat lonely without him, 'miss you Rufus', the mood
Drive past his house in Alex's car
Hope Rufus can hear us,
hear us whistle to him from that far.

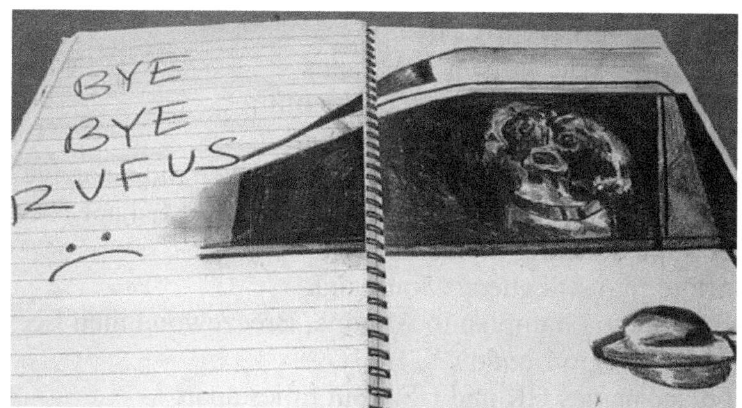

Figure 32
Still from poetry film *The Adventures of Rufus* by Lee Campbell (2024)

EPILOGUE

MICHAEL IN THE MOUNTAINS

Often the journey is more than the destination

The liminal journey
The space between
What is felt and what is seen
Through that window you peer out of is the window into yourself

This window between me and the Sussex rural wilderness
This stretch of track reminds me
Summer 1996
Buffalo towards Washington through the Appalachian mountains
Mum navigates, Dad drives
I, rear backseat passenger
Listening to R.E.M on cassette tape

Towards Eastbourne, early 2023
listening again to the same R.E.M tapes
Look up. Chalk man on the side of the hill
His name 'The long man of Wilmington'
No one knows how he got there. How and when did he arrive?
For me, there is only one man in the mountains, Michael
Michael Stipe queering my landscape
past Buffalo into Allegheny Mountains
to Ellicottville to Grampian to Altoona, Breezewood then Leesburg
then Washington to London
Shared place names UK and USA but miles apart
That separation allowed me to queer the landscape even more
During our road trip to discover rural America
A reality constructed in movies, I discovered me

When cowboys just happened to be strolling down Main Street
I noticed that the cut of the cowboy jean
makes for a tighter fit on bulging male butt cheek

Towards Eastbourne, I recall mental snapshots of rest stops,
motels and gas stations
Light illuminating certain parts of my journey
Glitchy like that of memory. Unstable, messy, slippery,
but my desire, I was certain

My landscape queered as I listen to Mr Stipe
I want to be seen, seen as me
But I don't want to be seen looking at he who I desire
I am watching, I am being watched over
Dad looking out the rear-view, behind him in the back window
And to get there he must see me in the foreground
But I was in the background
Hoping for when I could see and be seen seeing
I knew it would come but not sure how I would get there
How and when I would arrive.

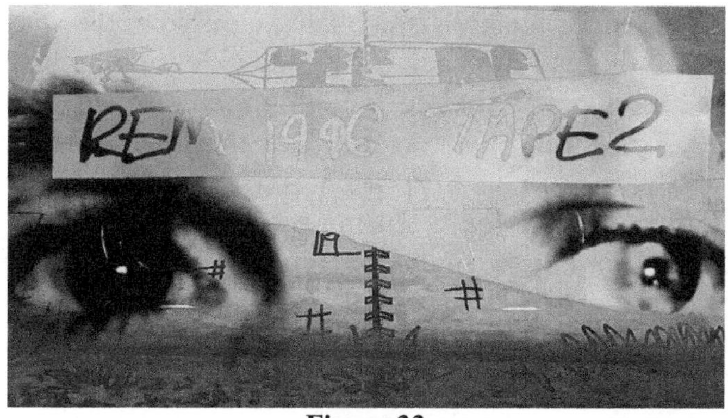

Figure 33
Still from poetry film *Michael in the Mountains* by Lee Campbell (2023)

TACTICS OF SEEING

A source of frustration, my school sex education
My elderly teacher although terribly kind
was not well prepared for a teenager's mind
Miss said, 'Andrew, this condom, roll it down this banana
I can hear giggles from someone. Is that you Pollyanna?'
Andrew struggled at first to get the sheath on
'Miss!', Jason shouted, 'Andrew's banana is two inches long!'
The default is hetero but what about gay?
I had a burning question for Miss but never dare say
It was quite unexpected but for me not so weird
when Miss in her 60s said she liked men with a beard
Wish I could go back now and tell Miss so do I
Nothing quite as sexy as a beard on a guy
Before the bell rang, just before class was over
'Miss', I wanted to say, 'I get my sex education from Mr Grover'
During his Religious Studies lessons, I'd sit at the back
My hands all over his beard and banana, me just imagining that

I'll never forget this cashier, she gave me such a dirty look
when she caught me buying *Playgirl* I hid inside a cookery book
I said, 'I'm buying it for my sister', I'm an only child in fact
I now laugh at things I did back then, I chuckle looking back
The nights I used to stay up late watching men for teenage girls
Make queer from straight just to feel back that I was in the world

Perfecting the art of the squint during a McDonald's stint
Escaping the gloom in the male changing room
Late 1994, first time I saw grammar school guy strip to his jock
I thought it rude not to glance what's under his pants
My eyes couldn't stop, my eyes were on lock
He had that grammar school voice my co-workers despise
So given worst job in the kitchen, he was stationed on fries

Every chance I'd be skipping me on burger flipping
Yet allowed me some spying at Grammar Guy frying
Getting sweaty whilst cooking, I couldn't stop looking
at Grammar School Guy through the flames of my griddle
Imagine a burger with his meat in the middle!

Then wanting to be a graphic designer,
I went to Pen and Ink in Tonbridge to work one school holiday
This guy called Jason made me blink. I wished that he were gay
He was the chief graphic designer, I had designs on him
His girlfriend though worked in payroll so chances very slim
When in came Beryl the tea lady with her usual jolly face
when she asked me 'Coffee or tea my dear?',
she saw me smiling over at Jase
Tell her I'm gay? No, not today. In fact, I'd never risk it
She'd spike my brew I'm telling you,
serve me poisoned tea and biscuit!
Everybody thinks that Beryl is this diamond hard to find
but this tea lady is downright shady. I read what's on her mind
'Well, if he's a graphic designer, he must gay
They're all arty farty those gays per se
I heard that on *Eastenders,* Barry and Colin kissed
I'm not saying I disapprove of benders, but I'm pleased
it's an episode that I missed. Now, would you like a digestive
with your tea Lee, or would you prefer a CREAM HORN?'
Before, I could give Beryl the measure of my mind,
her trolly and biscuits had gone
Smuggling copies of *Gay Times*
into my bedroom just to see guys like me
Creeping downstairs whilst parents asleep
to watch bad straight porn on Television X,
just to see a man naked.

From me as a teen, clever at not being seen
Fancying men, being called 'one of them'
George and Danny, all my teenage crushes
Sexy male schoolteachers, adrenaline rushes

Chelsea v Arsenal
Dad watched the match, I watched the players
Balls and sports, men in shorts
Football with Dad, both happy and sad
Dad watching one way, me quite the other
Nothing beats a good tackle seen undercover

I have learnt what it means to have a body,
to be a body, to inhabit the world here and now
See me through. No. See through me. No.
I am not that transparent, I am a body
A complex historied well
of senses, emotions, proximities, and encounters
A body that has learnt resilient being whilst
developing tactics of seeing
I would go back to former me and tell him
to prolong my stare at the handsome bear
and not in the least bit care

Queer is a community, anti-being controlled
Yet there are those of us who are persistently told
'YOU ARE TOO SLIM TO BE FAT!'
'YOU ARE TOO FAT TO BE THAT!'
When will we get over the labels and stereotypes
and just *be*?

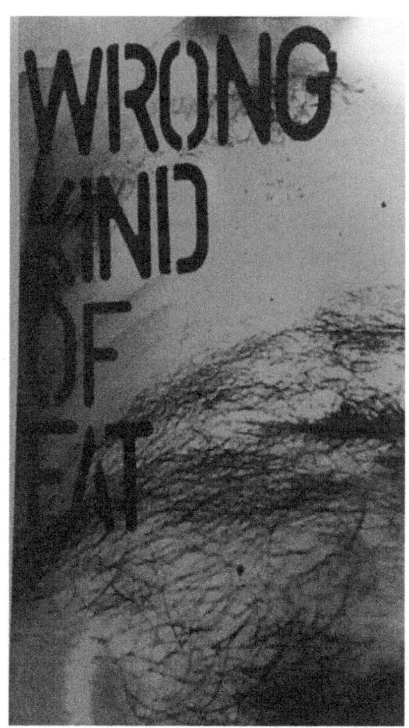

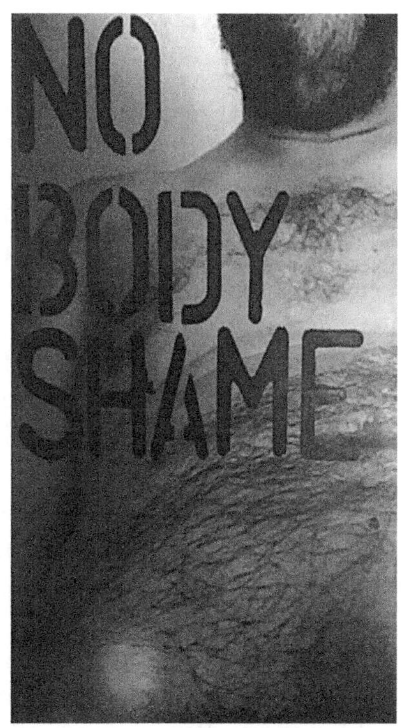

Figures 34 and 35
WRONG KIND OF FAT (2019) and *NO BODY SHAME* (2019)

To all the body gamers, shamers, namers and blamers
Don't define us guys by our bodily size
To the body police, we're flipping ginormous
What is obese, what is enormous
is the size of our talent to craft what we say
As poets, we're gallant at clever wordplay.

QUEERING THE LANDSCAPE

Bluebells stuck in-between toes of gay man laying alone in woods
Queering the landscape with every breath as leaves fall
Feeling an affinity with changing landscape
The liminal lure of woodland wonderlands
that appear unexpectedly in suburban sprawl.
Green hues paint their palette over concrete grey

Laying alone feeling in sync with the inherent queerness
in nature's cycle. Popular culture forgets, that in nature many
things cannot be easily taxonomised, reduced to signifiers

Queer as non-reductive gives possibility to dreaming and
imagining, living and breathing in pursuit of the realisation of
speculative queer ecologies

Queer people spend lifetimes coming out more than once in various
scenarios. We are bluebells wandering barefooted amongst
brambled thorn. When stung, when trampled over,
queer love is our dock leaf.

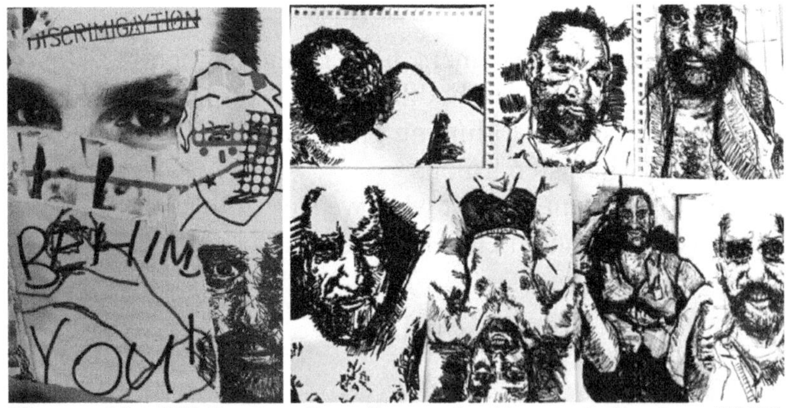

Figures 36 + 37 Mixed media collage and self-portrait drawings (2020)

CAMP (PART TWO)

Try educate the ignorant straight, doubt anybody could
Doubt Jack the lad does contemplate and why he ever should
learn all about queer history and those misunderstood
History shows 'gay' beyond Pride Day
and sex in Hampstead Wood
If you don't think true, Jack, your IQ is size of your manhood
when you told me, sure as can be,
'YOU GAYS HAVE NEVER HAD IT SO GOOD!'

These straights call themselves allies but in fact they've lied
They tick all those boxes to get discounts applied
Your fake allyship. Hypocrite! I simply cannot abide
Do me a favour, Mr Rainbow Flag Waver!
You reduced me to a sandwich, who the hell are you trying to kid?
Switching BLT with LBT just to make a few more quid
Pink-washing is not clever, however clever the word pun
Stick rainbow ice-cream up inside you where there's never ever sun

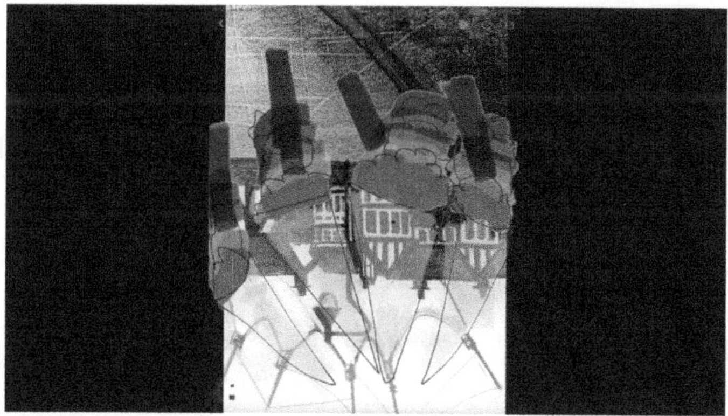

Figure 38 Still from poetry film *Camp* Lee Campbell (2023)

DOG BOY

Filthy animal within us all,
I am graffiti writing humour heckling DOG BOY!
Out tonight inflicting my scrawl
Pissing up against a wall
all over the palimpsest of the faded traces of words by other dogs
But this dog, my words are top
I am VACUNT
I am PRAWN COCKTAIL CRISPS
I am DOG BOY!

Polari taught me to be playfully covert in language
Yeah, nothing like cleaning his kitchen!
But DOG BOY is rude outright tonight
Won't beat around the bush
And even though my audience is public and ever changing,
my words are aimed right at you,
Sir.

When you shout,
'YOU TWO [MEN] CAN'T KISS',
DOG BOY shouts back,
'BOO HOO! HOO HISS! SCREW YOU! DON'T GIVE A PISS!'

I am DOG BOY!
I am Heckler!
Super Heckler!
Homo Heckler!
Vital agent in democratic exchange
Productive interrupter
One in the eye for politeness

Heckling
Shortest, briefest, neatest,
tidiest way of getting an idea across
DOG BOY heckles with finesse

Newsflash!
All systems dislocated
I am the stop
the pause
the break
within those smooth running
operations of homophobia
in your head
DOG BOY will derail you!
DOG BOY is queer
Gay man dog
Being queer
for you is a heckle
an interruption
Poetic, lyrical, unexpected, transformative interruptions
I must do this
I must interrupt the world
To save the world from you

Like a bolt out of the blue
Decapitating heteronormativity
Disrupting your commitment
to sequence,
to pattern,
to order everything
into a heteronormative box

Interruption from the Latin
'interrumpere'
(inter) 'between'
(rumpere) 'break'

We are Dog Boys, Hecklers, Super Hecklers, Homo Hecklers,
Protest Marching, Gobby Queer Insurgents
Puncture and prick in between spaces
We are Slapstickers. We get knocked down, but we survive
Heckling with homo humour!
Prick Up Your Ears!

SEE ME! SEE LEE! SEE DOG BOY!

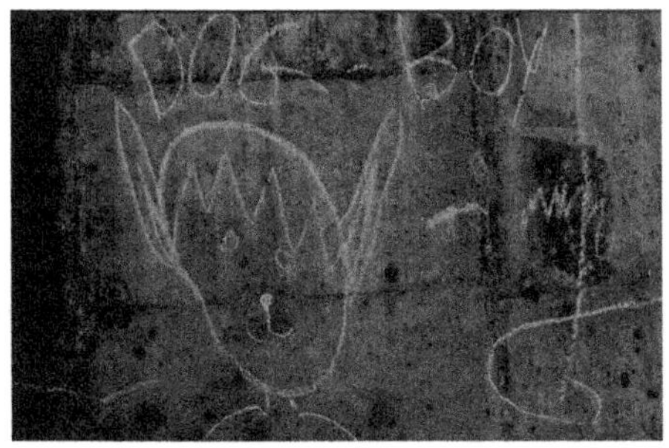

Figure 39 Still from film *DOG BOY* by Lee Campbell (2024)

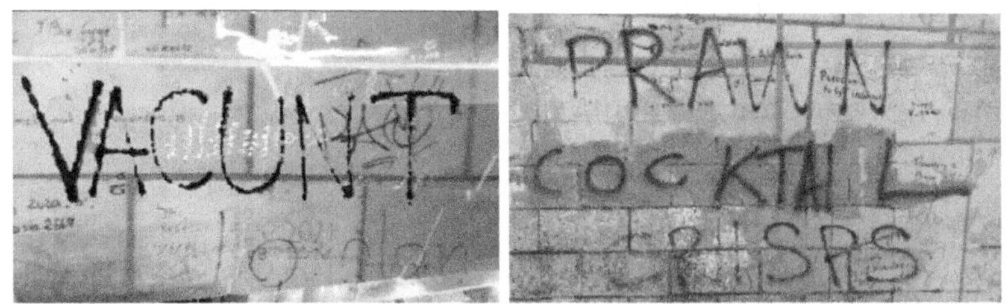

Figures 40 and 41
Stills from poetry film *DOG BOY* by Lee Campbell (2024)

Other excellent titles from London Poetry Books

Dark Matter.	*Amy Neilson Smith*
Joy Fear and F—K It	*Ant Smith*
There is a Tune	*Cathy Flower*
Pathways	*Anne Gaelan*
The Mirrors of Thespis	
Pocket full of Whispers	
Down Ghost Lane.	
Sky High Down to Ground	
Kissed by Honeybees.	*Keith Robert Bray*
English is a Foreign Language.	
Outside in Musing on Life,	
As an Autistic Poet	*Alain English*
Swimming with Endorphins.	*Fran Isherwood*
Ooetry	*Wendy Young*
Going with the Flow	
Making it Verse	
Rhymes for the Times	
The Scene of the Rhyme.	*Habiba Hrida*
I'm not here for your Entertainment.	*Tara Fleur*
Life and Hope	
Death Suicide Despair Poetry	*Jason Harris*
In the name of the Flesh	*Ernesto Sarezale*
The Bird of Morning.	
Of the Deep.	*IDF Andrew*
Twisted and Chewed	
Twisted and Chewed 2	*Shaun Rivers*
Running Through Trees and Glitter	*Rachael Chadwick*
Sniffing Glue and Playing	
Chicken on the M4	*Redeeming Features*

Printed and bound by CPI Group (UK) Ltd, Croydon, CR0 4YY

03/09/2024

01031595-0004